ASSASSINS BELOW

A GUILD TRILOGY
SHORT STORY COLLECTION

ASSASSINS BELOW

EMMA K. C. COUETTE

ELGIN HOUSE
— PRESS —

ALSO BY EMMA K. C. COUETTE

The Guild Trilogy:

Silent Night
Sacred Ruse
Solemn Vow
Assassins Below

The Fidalian Chronicles:

Summer's Revenge

AUTHOR'S NOTE

This novel is a collection of short stories set before, during, and after the events of the Guild Trilogy and, as such, contain spoilers for *Silent Night*, *Sacred Ruse*, and *Solemn Vow*. In order to enjoy these stories and the trilogy to the fullest, please follow the recommended reading order below.

Silent Night
One Fateful Night
One Fortunate Soul
Sacred Ruse
One Final Stand
One Fearful Choice
Solemn Vow
One Fatal Mistake
One Fragile Hope
One Fierce Devotion
One Fading Memory

TRIGGER WARNING

This book contains content/themes that may not be suitable for all readers, including: death, graphic violence, abuse, manipulation, death of a child, family trauma, and mental health issues such as anxiety and PTSD.
Please read at your own discretion.

To all those who, like me,
weren't ready to say goodbye yet.

ONE FATEFUL NIGHT

Haven City, 09/2104

Quinn

The street is cold and damp, the fog in the air so thick I can barely see my hand in front of my face. It's good weather for an assassination, in the sense that no one will be able to see if I slip up. On the other hand, I'll have a harder time noticing potential enemies on my tail. I shudder and dig my hands deeper into the pockets of my oversized cloak as I skirt around a puddle.

Despite the weather, my boots are still dry, and they'll need to stay that way if I want this to go according to plan. No wet footprints. No squeaky shoes. If I screw this up, I'll lose my hard-earned reputation, and I definitely won't get any closer to Agent One.

Haven is quiet at this time of night, or rather, this time in the morning. I stick to the edge of the buildings so I don't lose my way and count the streets as I cross them, careful to walk in a straight line. I'm getting close to my target now.

I've been watching the place for a week, and my entry plan is cemented in my head. Approach from the side of the corner lot, slip through the garden gate—which has lovely oiled hinges—sneak behind the hedge that halves the yard to the side of the house, and get in through the first-floor window that's always unlocked.

Piece of cake.

As long as the damned fog doesn't lead me to the wrong house.

It'll be fine, I tell myself. *You're Silent Night. You can do this.*

I allow myself a small smile and then cross the road to the fateful street.

Jax

The clock on the wall says it's nearing three in the morning, but I can't sleep. The house is too quiet, and I keep thinking I see shadows in the thick fog outside my window. I tell myself it's just the maple tree, but I can't quite bring myself to believe it.

It's the time of day where nightmares come to life and people disappear without cause.

I groan and roll away from the window.

You've been reading too many of Blake's horror novels, I chide myself. *Nothing is going to happen tonight.*

Again, it's hard to listen, but it's the most logical explanation. I should've said no when Blake recommended that ghost book, but Bast never would've let me hear the end of it. I'm not sure saving my pride is worth sacrificing my sleep though. We have a big test tomorrow, and I'm going to flunk it at this rate.

I roll over again and sit up, staring out the window as I rub at my temples. I want to wake Mom up and ask her to make me a glass of warm milk, but I'm too old for that now, and she won't be any good to Jenson tomorrow if I wake her at this hour.

There's a thick fog hanging over the city tonight, enough that I can't see the hedge in our backyard, though it stands only ten feet from my window. The thought unnerves me, and I get to my feet, taking a few steps until I'm standing at the window.

The early morning breeze rushes in and rustles my t-shirt, sending shivers down my spine.

Just go back to bed, I tell myself. *Who cares if you can't see the hedge?*

I should listen to myself, seeing as getting up didn't help matters any, but I linger a moment longer, squinting into the night. The world seems too quiet beyond my window, as if the city is holding its breath.

Then an owl hoots somewhere above the house, and I nearly jump out of my skin at the sound. By the time I recognize what it is, my heart is racing.

Still, it breaks the tension, and I'm laughing at myself a moment later, hand pressed against my chest as I lean against the windowsill to catch my breath.

Oh man, if Bast and Blake could see me now…

I smile to myself and am just about to turn back to bed when I see a shadow pass beneath my window, half hidden by the fog.

Quinn

When I reach the hedge looming in the fog, I know I've chosen the right yard. The quiet backyard gate was my first indication, but this *Molly Forrester* can't be the only person in Haven who actually takes care of her house. I wonder if anyone will tend to it when she's dead and gone or if it'll become just another house lost to time.

I pass by so many crumbling buildings every day, homes fallen victim to neglect and history. Sometimes, I wonder who they belonged to, and if those people would mourn their passing, but it's not worth my worry. Everything must die, eventually.

Tonight, it's Molly's turn; one more Resistance Agent being sent to the grave where they belong.

I creep along the shadow of the hedge as I approach the shed, trying to keep out of view of the windows. Though it's three in the morning, you can't be too careful when it comes to the Resistance. There's a reason we haven't killed the bastards yet; too clever for their own good.

It wouldn't be pleasant to come face to face with her, awake in the living room, waiting for my appearance, especially not when I'm supposed to kill without being seen or heard.

Of course, no one ever lives to tell the tale of our encounter, but I like to lend truth to the stories people weave about my kills. I like to *be* the Silent Night they all know and fear. What's the point of building a reputation if you don't live up to it?

I'm smiling to myself as I dart from behind the hedge and to the side of the house, pressing my back up against the brick. I don't dare look up at the windows above me. If anyone *is* watching, any sudden movement this close to the house will alert them of my presence right away.

I wait the space of five breaths and then I take a step closer to my chosen window entrance, careful not to scrape any weapons against the house. Patience is key in a situation like this, which a lot of my fellow assassins lack. A slow kill is a good kill; speed makes you sloppy.

It takes me a few minutes to inch the ten feet to the first-storey window, and I wait a few more before I turn around and peer into the room inside. Pitch black greets me, and when my eyes finally adjust, I can just make out some furniture—a short table, a couple chairs, and a couch.

Living room, I tell myself.

What room it is doesn't matter as much as the fact that it's empty, though.

I grin.

This will be easy.

I dig my fingernails under the bottom of the window and pull it up, moving slowly in case it squeaks, but it's just as quiet as the back gate, and I slide it all the way up without a sound.

I crawl through it with ease and find myself standing alone in Molly Forrester's living room with no one the wiser. There's a silence to the space that other people would find eerie, but I consider it peaceful, a nice break from the cacophony of the Guild.

That's what I like the most about my missions, being able to find pockets of silence within the mad rush of my life, being able to find a touch of freedom.

I take a deep breath to steady myself and then set out in search of the staircase.

Jax

I want to believe the shadow was just a figment of my imagination, going wild because of the fog and my restless night, but something keeps me from giving in. I have a feeling in my gut that if I ignore this, I'll regret it forever.

I stay standing at the window, my eyes glued to the spot beneath me where I last saw the anomaly. The chill of the night has set into my bones now, and I shiver despite myself. Autumn is starting to set in. It'll soon be time to bring my sweaters out of the closet again.

Ten minutes pass and in them, I see nothing else, not even the owl that scared me earlier. I should go back to bed, should dismiss it as another dream, but I turn away from the window and head for my bedroom door.

The clock on the wall says it's a quarter to four now, and I groan at the thought, but some things are more important than passing a history test. Some things will haunt you for the rest of your life if you turn your back on them.

I slip on a pair of socks before I go, so my feet won't stick to the hardwood floor and alert a possible intruder of my presence. I also grab my handgun from my dresser drawer and stick it in the waistband of my pajama pants, just in case. You can never be too careful in this damn city.

The doorknob is like ice in my hand, but I ignore the shock of it as I ease the door open. It creaks sometimes, but if you open it just right, you can avoid it. I slip through it when I have enough room to do so comfortably, and swing it shut again, careful not to let it bang on the door jamb. I stop it just shy of clicking into place and slip down the hall.

The house seems to breathe around me, as if I can hear every beam and floorboard shifting in the night, settling in for the long winter ahead. Every shadow in the upstairs hall looks like an assassin ready to jump me. I want to rub my eyes to clear away the images, but I'm afraid to look away, afraid of what I'll see when I look back.

My steps are slow but sure as I take the time to avoid the squeaky floorboards between my room and Mom's, passing the bathroom and the study on my way. I half hoped to see a light on in the study, Mom still up reading or poring over notes from Jenson, but the door is shut tight.

Mom's bedroom is at the end of the hall, normally accentuated by the moonlight streaming in through the lone hall window to the right of her door, but the fog is too heavy for that tonight. Still, my eyes have adjusted to the dark enough to see that her door is ajar.

A weight settles in my chest.

She never leaves her door open, says it's only an invitation for all the things that go bump in the night.

Something is very wrong.

Quinn

Molly's bedroom is lit only by the dull light seeping in through her open curtains. The fog outside is beginning to lift, and I know I must carry out my task quickly. Her bed stands in the middle of the far wall, and I cross a woven area rug to reach her. She's sleeping deeply, curled up on her side. For a second, I pity her. She'll be gone before she notices the danger, but that's a blessing, the only one I'll ever give.

I draw my rapier out of my hip sheath in one long movement, careful not to make a sound. The blade is razor sharp; I spent the afternoon making it that way. Anything less than perfect and Molly will have too much time to contemplate her demise.

I wait a few more moments to make sure my presence hasn't stirred her, and then I creep up to the bed and raise the knife above her head, lining the point up with the soft skin just behind her main artery.

I'll get one shot at this. If I do it right, it'll be over shortly. If not... Well, let's just say things might get messy.

I count my heartbeats in the silent room as I steady myself. Then I plunge the blade down into her neck, through the other side, and push. The rapier rips through the front of her throat, and blood gushes onto the sheets. I ignore it as I use both hands to hold her flailing body against the bed until it stills.

Another job well done.

I roll Molly onto her back then and check her pulse. The gaping wound in her neck should be proof enough, but I never like to assume. That's how mistakes are made, and in my line of work, they can be fatal.

My fingers find no pulse, and I slide my rapier back into its sheath, satisfied with myself.

Molly Forrester is dead.

A shudder runs through my body, but I ignore the awful feeling that comes with it. Now is not the time to feel the weight of my latest sin. I have to get out of here first.

Still, I tuck the woman's name into the back of my mind for later, vowing to never forget her.

The sky is clear of fog when I turn back to the window, and I know it's time to go. Days end, people die, and life moves on. There's nothing we can do to change that.

I slip silently to the window and slide the lock over before wrenching it open without a sound.

I'm halfway through it when I hear the faint sound of the door swinging open behind me.

Jax

The first thing I notice when I open the door to my mother's bedroom is the smell of fresh blood, and my heart clenches in my chest. The second thing I notice is the girl straddling Mom's windowsill.

She's dressed all in black, from her boots to her cloak, and her hood is thrown back to reveal long, dark locks and a pale face. She can't be any older than me, and yet…

She killed my mother.

It only takes a quick look at the bed to confirm that. Mom is lying limp in the sheets, her throat torn wide open and her eyes staring at me without seeing.

She's gone. I'll never hear her sing again while she makes pancakes in the morning or listen while she rants about something Jenson said.

I suddenly find it very hard to breathe, so I look back to the girl.

Assassin, I remind myself. *She's the enemy.*

Instinct tells me to reach for the pistol in my pants and shoot her, but something makes me pause.

Maybe it's her age, the thought that she's just another stupid kid like me. Maybe it's the fear of missing and having to fend off her inevitable counterattack.

But maybe it's the way she's staring at me like a deer caught in the light beam of the train. I've never seen such raw fear in someone's eyes before, and it chills me to the bone, freezes me to the spot.

She doesn't want to have to kill me, I realize. And I don't want to have to kill her.

I take a deep breath and decide to let her go, despite everything screaming at me to cut her down where she stands. I raise my hands above my head and back away, taking slow steps toward the door.

She watches me go like an animal curious about a new discovery, and I don't take my eyes off of her until the door shuts between us with a click.

I fall to my knees in front of the door and rest my head against it as the tears finally come, as I curse myself for what I've done. My mother is dead, and I let her assassin go.

Never again.

Quinn

When the door shuts behind the boy, I don't stick around to ask questions. I drop out of the window like it's on fire and scurry down to the yard, breaking into a sprint for the back gate.

If I had known Molly Forrester had a child, I would've been more careful, I wouldn't have lingered.

You should've been more careful regardless, I chide myself. *A stupid stunt like that could've gotten you killed.*

By all rights, it should have.

I saw the pistol tucked into his pants. He could have shot me so easily, but he hesitated. He walked away. He let me go.

If I live to be a hundred, I may never understand it, but I recognize his sacrifice. It's the only reason I didn't kill him too. The Charger will kill me himself if he finds out I was seen, if he finds out I let the witness walk free, but a part of me doesn't care. It wasn't that boy's time.

If his name ever graces my list, I won't hesitate, but tonight, we both get to live. Tonight, we get another chance to see where Haven City will take us.

ONE FORTUNATE SOUL

Haven City, 03/2108

Bast

As the train rolls into the outskirts of the city, I check the clock on the wall and suppress a groan.

It's only three-thirty?

I feel like I've been on this damned train for days, and I still have two and a half hours before I can call it quits on work.

The ride has been uneventful so far, which is both a blessing and a curse. On the one hand, I'm not bleeding or dead from an assassin's blade. On the other hand, I'm bored out of my mind. It wouldn't be so bad if I had more than boxes of food for company, and maybe some playing cards, but the cramped car offers no form of entertainment, so I stare out the small window and watch the houses whir by.

The train is starting to slow now, preparing for its stop at the station, and I can see my surroundings more clearly. It's a nice change from the endless green of the farms. Open spaces kind of give me the creeps after so long in the Resistance.

Sure, I can see the assassins coming, but there's nowhere for me to hide either.

The P.A. system clicks on then, and a message blares out from the cracked speaker above the door of my car. "All personnel prepare for our final stop. We will be arriving at the station in five minutes, at precisely three-forty in the afternoon. The train will remain stopped for twenty minutes to unload cargo before leaving the station again at four o'clock to return to the farms. Thank you."

The P.A. system clicks off, and I take a moment to mock the man's stuffy voice before dragging myself to my feet. It's time to do some actual work, and I'm not bummed about it. In fact, my butt could use the activity. The damned metal floor has turned it to pins and needles.

I do a couple stretches to get the blood flowing again while I wait for the train to reach the station. It's moving at a snail's pace now, and I count down the seconds in my head. Then I clamp my hands over my ears just as it screeches to a halt.

Man, I hate that sound.

It chills me to the bone.

I shake my head to clear it and head to the door of my car. The food got to Haven in one piece, and now we have to make sure the assassins aren't going to attack the train in town this time. You can never be too careful with the sneaky bastards. They're always one step ahead, so we've got to be at least three ahead if we want to get the advantage.

I yank the door open, sending some rust flying, and hop down between the train platform and the railroad coupling holding my car to the next. I wait in the shadows, drawing my crossbow from its holder across my back and scanning the crowd for anything suspicious. All down the train my fellow soldiers are doing the same.

Nothing seems out of place at first glance, just the regular workers in their tattered brown uniforms waiting to unload the train and some street kids mingling about the yard, hoping to snatch some dinner. Still, I wait for the signal before stepping onto the platform. It comes a second later, a long blast of the horn followed by two short ones.

My fellow soldiers and I take our places at the side of the train cars as the workers approach, keeping our weapons held at the ready. I watch as a small team of five blends into the crowd to search the surrounding area for any lurking assassins.

I keep my bow at the ready, but as the minutes drag on with not so much as a toe out of place, my thoughts drift to other things, namely my plans for after my shift. Jax promised to meet me at the Den tonight around six o'clock for a game of cards with some other agents, and I'm determined to win, though it shouldn't be hard. All I have to do is choose which trick deck to bring.

I smirk.

Jax would kill me if he found out I'm cheating, but it's not for his benefit. I wouldn't do it if it was just one-on-one; I wouldn't need to. Jax is great at a lot of things, but playing cards is not one of them. I doubt he could win if I cheated in his favour. Still, it's fun to have him there. He's one of the few people who doesn't underestimate me, and I wish I could have the same quiet confidence in myself.

Hai

It is a beautiful day to kill someone. The sun is high in the sky, the air is warm with the first signs of spring, and there isn't a cloud in sight. I throw my head back and breathe in the heavy scent of opportunity, a grin snaking its way onto my face.

Yes, a wonderful day to spill blood.

Beneath where I'm crouched behind a chimney stack, the train station is bursting with life as the raggedy workers make haste unloading the latest shipment from the farms. I can't tell what food is in them from this distance, but I'm not after it anyway. The Guild has plenty of food left for the month.

No, I'm after a particular Resistance agent.

I sneer at the long line of grey guarding the train, as if their puny force could stop us if we really wanted that food. We have taken it by force again and again, and yet, the Resistance can't seem to get the message. They always return, and I don't know if it speaks more to their bravery or their stupidity.

Doesn't matter anyway, they'll all be dead someday.

There's a certain joy in watching them struggle in vain, a certain splendour to their wasted lives.

I smile and search up and down the line for my quarry. Their grey uniforms make them blend in with one another, but I'm looking for someone with a crossbow. The weapon is rarer than guns these days, though the criteria only narrows my options down to three.

I groan and run a hand through my hair.

There are two possible solutions to my problem: get close enough to discern the potential victims' appearances, or just kill them all.

I know which one is more fun.

I glance at the clock tower to the west of the station as I mull over my decision. Only fifteen more minutes until the train leaves again and I miss my window. It's time to get to work. With one last look around the square, I leave my spot by the chimney and start looking for the easiest way to the street.

Bast

Fifteen minutes left, but I know it will feel like an eternity. It always seems like the workers move in slow motion, and I wish someone could invent something to make the process smoother, but innovation died years ago in this forsaken city, and automation would take away one of the only things giving these people meaning in their lives.

Not for the first time, I wish we could take some of them back with us, to make their lives better than this endless monotony and struggle to survive, but I know we can't. Any one of them could be assassins in disguise, and this war is already going badly enough without inviting the damn bastards into our home.

Still, it pains me to see them in their threadbare clothes with hardly any fat on their bones while I stand here in my impeccable uniform, knowing I'm going home to a warm bed and a nice meal.

Seeing the street kids hurts even more because I once stood in their shoes, and even though I've found salvation for myself, I can't do a damn thing to help them.

My hands shake with anger, and I bite my tongue to steady myself.

Nothing good comes from worrying about it, I remind myself. *Your anger helps no one.*

I avert my gaze from the square for a moment to clear my head, hoping the sight of the blue sky will calm me down, but then I catch sight of a figure dressed all in black on a rooftop across the street. As he turns in place, the sun glints off the long, curved sword strapped against his back.

Assassin.

I almost drop my bow as I fumble for the small whistle in my breast pocket and give it three long blows. As the shrill sound echoes through the station and up and down the line, my fellow agents raise their weapons and prepare themselves for an attack.

I raise my bow and aim a bolt at the assassin on the roof.

Hai

The hairs on my neck run vertical as the whistle reverberates in my ear drums, signalling danger. The Resistance knows I'm here, but it matters not. It only adds to the fun, the challenge, and I never walk away from a good fight.

I don't look back towards the square, knowing the agents won't dare to leave their posts and that I'll be out of sight before they can bring me down anyway. This house has attic access to the roof, and once I cross the peak, I'll be out of range.

I'm only a few steps away from my spot at the chimney when something whizzes past my leg and clatters to the roof, sliding down the shingles until it drops out of sight.

I grin.

You missed.

Still, I turn, despite myself, to see who took the shot, and find one of the crossbowmen staring intently at me.

Brave soul, but it won't be enough to spare him. He's just won himself the first spot on my kill list, and I intend to make his death worth my while. I intend to paint the railroad tracks with his blood.

No one shoots at me and lives to tell the tale; I can't have anyone ruining my reputation. Silent Night may have stolen my place as heir, but she won't steal my place as Agent One, no one will. Anyone who so much as threatens my power will meet a violent and bloody end.

Bast

My bolt misses the assassin's knee by an inch, and I curse under my breath, even as I hurry to reload. The one disadvantage of crossbows is how painful it is to take two shots in succession, not to mention how hard it is to rack the weapon without looking.

I don't dare take my eyes off my quarry, though, worried he might vanish into thin air. The assassins are masters at that. There one second and gone the next like they were never there in the first place.

Before I can finish reloading, the assassin does something unexpected; he turns and looks at me. Even from a distance, his gaze is lethal, like the strike of a viper. I can feel his hatred and distaste for me, and everyone around me. The sensation makes me want to look away, but I ignore the urge and try to memorize his features instead. Jenson will want to know what he looked like, though it's hard to see much from this far away. All I can say for certain is that he's blond.

He smiles at me before turning on his heel and walking out of range, and the sight freezes me to the spot, keeping me from firing my second shot at his exposed back.

It's a smile that says, *You made a mistake.*

Hai

I slip through the roof hatch and tear through the house below in a slow-motion hurricane, my mind howling for blood even as my body remains calm, stoic, ever the invisible assassin.

The street outside is empty, everyone lured away by the arrival of the train and the Resistance's warning whistle. I'm not naive enough to trust that I'm alone, though. I know the grey coats have some agents mulling about the adjacent streets, on the lookout for tainted souls just like me.

I'm not going to do anything about it though. You see, knowing is almost the entire battle. It takes away half the fun, but they'll be hard-pressed to catch me, and if they do manage it, they won't live long enough to realize their folly, to regret their stupidity. I may not have a title, but I have plenty to be feared for.

I sneak through the streets like I'm out for a Sunday stroll, and it doesn't take long for me to skirt around the square and materialize behind the train, watching the station from behind the scenes, from within the shadows.

The Resistance really should learn to watch their backs.

I walk through the gravel of the train yard, kicking up dust and stones, as I count the railcars, looking for number twenty-seven. The shooter should be between it and twenty-eight, likely still searching for a glimpse of me on the rooftops.

I laugh to myself.

How innocent these Resistance *soldiers* are, how tiresome.

My eyes lock on the twenty-seventh car then, and a grin crackles across my lips like a shot of lightning.

Finally, time for some fun.

We'll see how long this worm lasts before I crush him beneath my boot.

Bast

As soon as the assassin steps out of view, I'm on the move, abandoning my post on instinct, and heading behind the long line of rail cars. I'm not as good at strategy as Blake or Jax, but I didn't finish my training early because my teachers felt bad for me. I know how the assassins think, to a certain extent, and if I was as obviously bloodthirsty as that guy, I would sneak up on my prey from behind.

Nothing better than scaring the shit out of your victim first, right?

So I grip my loaded crossbow and drift down the train further until I come to a stand of barrels. Two are loaded with ropes and other supplies, and one is turned on its side, spilling sand into the already dusty gravel yard.

I decide it's the perfect spot and get down onto my stomach with the bow pointed above the sideways barrel, the bolt just barely visible to someone passing by. It's a vulnerable position, lying prone like this, but it gives me the best chance of remaining undetected. As long as I don't have to get up in a hurry, I'll be fine.

Probably.

I lay in wait as the chatter of the yard slowly recedes into a low hum in the background.

Just when I'm about to search for another vantage point, he appears, walking into the yard from a side street like he owns the place. His confidence is startling; I've never seen an assassin walk in the open like that. Still, the circumstances couldn't be better, even if they are a little strange.

This assassin will be dead before he knows what hit him.

My finger flexes on the trigger of my bow, and just as I'm about to let the bolt fly, an explosion wracks the yard, lighting up the sky in a massive blaze of grey and orange.

Hai

I take another step forward when a sound like breaking glass fills the air and the railcar in front of me goes up in smoke and flame.

The force of the explosion sends me flying backward into the gravel, the impact dazing me for a moment before I can regain my bearings. Car twenty-seven looks like a funeral pyre, and I can hear soldiers and station workers alike screaming in the square as they try to work together to put it out.

My hands sting, and I scowl at the cuts marring their already scarred surface.

Nothing hurts me anymore but me, but my memories and wayward thoughts.

I shakily get to my feet and dust myself off before stumbling forward a few steps, unsure of how to proceed. It's a strange feeling for me, one that settles in the pit of my stomach like a rock attempting to pull me down into the depths of my own personal abyss, but I ignore it. This is only temporary confusion.

Logic says the explosion should've killed the crossbow man I'm after, but intuition tells me the answer is not so simple, and I listen to it. It's the instinct that has kept me alive all these years at the Guild, after all, always one step ahead of my enemies and three steps ahead of my friends.

So I yield to the hairs rising on my neck and turn around, searching the train yard around me as the railcar continues to burn. I can already feel the heat, and I'm glad I did not wear my cloak today.

The yard is almost boring in its simplicity, in its emptiness, but a gathering of barrels about a dozen yards to my right gives me pause. It would be the perfect place for a…

Ambush.

I drop to the ground like a flightless bird just before I hear the unmistakable click of a crossbow being fired.

Bast

The assassin hits the ground so fast, I don't have time to redirect my shot, and the bolt goes clean over his head, missing him again. This time, I don't stop to contemplate it or reload my weapon. Instead, I jump to my feet, throw the crossbow aside, and start sprinting for the safety and chaos of the square.

I don't know who set off that explosion—if it was assassins or an accident—but anything will be safer than this empty rail yard right now.

Anything.

I can't tell if he's following me, but I don't look back, not until I've rounded the corner of a railcar ten yards up and reached the safety of the main square. Then I pull my small pistol out of my coat and keep my back pressed along the railcar as I walk down it and scan the area.

The fire is still raging, but someone was smart enough to disengage the adjacent cars to stop it from spreading further. I watch as a long line of workers and Resistance agents pass a series of pails back and forth towards the blaze. The pinch of water barely makes it sputter, but I guess it's better than nothing, the best we can do really.

It'll die down once it runs out of fuel, and if nothing else, it'll keep the street kids warm tonight.

It also means my job here is done, seeing as I can't rightly escort a burning half-train back to the farms. Running for my life is probably a good excuse to shirk my duties, right?

I try to laugh, but my hand is shaking, almost going numb from how tightly I'm holding my gun.

Man, what I wouldn't give to have Jax and Blake here right now.

Everything is always so much easier with them, but I know that sometimes you have to do hard things alone. Sometimes life gives you no choice, and it's moments like these where heroes are made or broken.

I take a deep breath and steady my hand.

You can do this.

My steps are more sure now as I make my way closer to the centre of the station, where the remaining Resistance soldiers are huddled together. My eyes are still frantically scanning my surroundings though, just waiting for the assassin to resurface. There's no way he's going to let me go after I shot at him twice, unless that explosion did more damage than it seemed.

I'm a few yards away from the group when one of them turns in my direction, a woman with long, black hair and a black and red cloak.

It's Trey, Avery's second.

What on earth is she doing here?

"Oh my God," she breathes. "Sebastian Foster?"

I grimace at the name but try to keep my emotions in check as she rushes toward me, her heeled boots clicking on the concrete beneath them.

"Holy shit, it is you," she says as she stops in front of me and looks me up and down. "We thought you were dead."

I frown, lowering my pistol. "What? Why?"

"That explosion hit car twenty-seven, the one you were supposed to be guarding. How did you get away?"

"I… I left my post before the explosion. There was an assassin on the roof across the square earlier, and I took a shot at him and missed. I figured he would come after me, so I made sure I wasn't in the last place he saw me."

Trey narrows her eyes. "What did he look like?"

I shrug. "I didn't really get a good look at him, but he had blond hair and an ugly look in his eyes. Not really someone you want to mess with."

"The fucking bastard," she says, almost to herself. Then she looks me in the eye. "This was my fault. I was tracking that assassin earlier today but lost him about an hour ago. I had no idea he would show up here. They called me for back-up after the train exploded."

"You did the best you could. Too bad I couldn't have killed him for you or led him right to you. I didn't think he would give up on me that easily."

Trey shakes her head. "He knows better than to attack you with all these people around, especially now that he knows I'm here. We have a…history, you could say."

I raise an eyebrow. "What kind of history?"

"One that's none of your business," she replies, "though it's certainly not the kind you're thinking of so get your mind out of the damned gutter. Honestly… "

I shrug. "You said it, not me."

She just rolls her eyes and turns away. "Come on, let's meet up with the others and get you back to the Resistance before another assassin tries to murder you. I do not want to have to explain to Ajax how you died on my watch."

I grin. "Now where would be the fun in that?"

She ignores me, and I follow her away from the train, glad I dodged the bullet and get to live one more day. Still, I turn to look behind me as we join the others, not entirely convinced the mystery assassin won't shoot me in the back from the shadows. All he needs is a clear shot and an escape route, and he can be gone before the others even realize I'm dead.

The thought crawls through me, and I don't put my pistol away. I'm going to need a long, hard drink when I get back to the Warehouse, to clear my head and help me sleep tonight, something to make me forget the look in that assassin's eyes that promised endless pain.

Hai

I watch the Resistance agents regroup and file out of the train station towards the north, splitting into groups of twos and threes in order to confuse assassins on their tail.

A burning anger rages through me as Trey falls into step beside my lost quarry, knowing that this time, I will have to accept defeat. I would give anything to wrap my hands around her traitorous neck and squeeze until the light in her eyes blinks out, but there are rules I must follow until told otherwise.

She is not to be harmed, at least not by me.

And the funny thing is that she doesn't even know. She doesn't realize that Father's words are the only thing keeping her safe right now, a notion so ironic I might be sick. She doesn't deserve Father's protection. She doesn't deserve to live, and yet here she is, prancing around in her fancy robes and pretending she isn't a monster like the rest of us.

One day, she'll live to regret her betrayal, and I hope that when she begs for her life, her killer doesn't even consider giving her mercy.

I hope she dies alone and afraid, and I hope I'm there to see it.

ONE FINAL STAND

Haven City, 08/2110

Trey

The wind whips through my dark hair as I lay prone against the hillside, watching the dilapidated building across the dirt road. Its walls shudder against the weight of the impending storm, but I know it's just for show. The Barn has more chance of surviving a hurricane than I do, let alone a thunderstorm. Still, the sight is eerie, and I risk a glance behind me for the sixth time in the past twenty minutes.

Any good assassin knows that's not the smartest tactic, but I haven't been a true assassin in a long time, and I never followed the rules anyway.

I sigh and brush my hair out of my face. I haven't seen anything of note yet, but I know that means next to nothing. If my suspicions are right and the assassins really are here, they're not going to be using the front door. Then again, that could be exactly what they want me to believe.

I clench my fists and bury my face in the grass.

Did you really think it would be that easy? Did you really think you could be the hero?

Overhead, the clouds are darkening, and I can hear thunder rumbling in the distance, closer to the Warehouse. My chest tightens when I think of it, when I think of Quinn left behind, again, with not much of an explanation.

Is she worried about me? Is she mad I left? Does she still hate me?

Part of me believes she could never truly hate me, but pain does terrible things to people.

I should know.

I hope that whatever happens, I can make it back to her, that I'll get a chance to prove myself, to mend the broken bond between us. I hope Kuen is taking care of her when I cannot.

I snort at that.

I'll be lucky if the man doesn't come after me, guns blazing, for this crazy stunt. He knows better than Quinn how reckless I can be. I'd be dead several times over without him, though I still don't understand why someone like him would think I'm worth the risk.

I take a deep breath and lift my head again, slowly so the sudden movement doesn't alert anyone to my presence. In retrospect, my red and black cape was probably not the best wardrobe choice, but I was hoping nothing would be amiss and I could walk down the halls as Avery's Second again, though I know it's a high hope.

The sick feeling in my stomach won't let me believe it.

Thunder booms in the sky, much closer this time, and I suppress a shudder. I'm not afraid of storms, but it's a bad omen, and rain makes it so much harder to travel undetected. Not to mention the fact that I'll get completely soaked in no time flat laying in this long grass.

I suppress a groan and shift my weight to my left side, flexing my hip to ward off the growing stiffness. It's been almost half an hour now and there's been no sign of Resistance agents or assassins.

Maybe the place is empty.

And maybe Sephtis Aeron is misunderstood too.

I crack a smile. There's nothing better than poking fun at the old man, except maybe getting the chance to slit his throat.

I'm considering moving to a different vantage point when I notice movement on the far side of the field.

My eyes snap up and zero in on the figure sneaking through the grass towards the Barn. He's dressed head to toe in grey, in what can only be a Resistance uniform. The sight should comfort me. I should let out a sigh of relief and relax the tension in my muscles.

There's only one problem.

I recognize that man, and he is most certainly *not* a Resistance agent.

Anane

The cell is dark, and the smell of iron from earlier is still thick in the air, but I ignore it all and count the seconds in my head. My salvation will come soon, and they will all be sorry they didn't kill me when they had the chance.

Silent Night went to great lengths to keep me chained, and I do admire her effort to a certain extent, but it won't be enough. She made the mistake of thinking Father is no longer on my side, but that couldn't be further from the truth.

If he didn't want me to get caught, I would've been dead already. I would've begged for death, and I think she knows that, somewhere in that bleeding heart of hers. I think that's what scares her.

And so it should.

I grin as I watch the flames in the torches flicker, sending warped shadows across my guards' faces. They'll be nothing but flesh and blood soon, nothing but thread in a tapestry of violence, but it's for a good cause.

I've been sent to bring Silent Night and the Resistance to their knees in sorrow, and I will not disappoint. I can't.

If I don't play my part perfectly, Father will have my head, and besides, it's what I was born to do, all I know how to do. There's no point wasting talent that is rightfully earned.

Further in the dungeons, I hear someone start to scream, and I know that's my cue. I open the still-healing wound on my arm with a slice of my thumbnail and start scrawling my message on the wall behind me.

Trey

As the first drop of rain hits my nose and runs down my face, the assassin walks closer to the Barn in his stolen uniform, except a part of me knows it's not stolen. I wouldn't be here at all if I didn't suspect, even just for a moment, that the Barn had been compromised. This man proves me at least partially right, but I won't know how deep the deception goes until I get inside.

I want to believe that Quinn was wrong about our uncle, that he is not a part of this sinister plot, but I can't bring myself to do it. Still, everyone deserves to be considered innocent until proven guilty, even if they wouldn't extend the same kindness to you.

As the assassin ducks through the tattered door of the barn, I make my move, giving a final scan of the area before I push myself up into a crouch. Then I take slow, deliberate steps towards the Barn, using the tall grass as cover. The rain starts to fall more earnestly, and I pray I can make it inside before the skies really open up.

It takes me ten minutes to reach the flaky, pink walls of the Barn, but it's worth the effort to be sure I haven't been spotted. The real test will be whether or not the assassin is still waiting in the entrance. I'll have to kill him if he is, which would be a real waste of time and energy. I wouldn't regret his death, but killing assassins is not my mission today, unfortunately.

I take a deep breath and pull my dagger out of my pocket, steeling myself for an encounter. Then I inch along the barn wall to the door and slip inside.

My ears strain to hear any movement as my eyes work to adjust to the darkness. They must've cut the power to this room, which means there probably aren't any security cameras either. Still, I pull my collar up over my face just in case. It only takes a few moments to deduce that I'm alone, and I relax my stance a little.

Now for the fun part.

I'm not stupid enough to take the stairs down into the base. I don't want to explain myself to the regular guards if my suspicions are wrong. If I'm right, the place will be crawling with assassins and I'll be locked away before I can warn Quinn and the others.

So I have to play my cards right, and luckily, being Avery's Second gave me plenty of options, plenty of insider knowledge.

I stalk over to the far side of the room, careful to keep my footsteps light in case there is someone listening beneath the trap door leading to the staircase. The two feet around the perimeter of the entrance are usually cast in shadow, the light not reaching them. No one notices the hatch in the wall, or if they do, they dismiss it as a regular air vent.

This air vent happens to be my usual entrance and exit. Old assassin habits die hard, and I hated the idea of the guards downstairs documenting my comings and goings, so one of the first things I did when I arrived was find another way out. It looks like my paranoia is finally paying off.

I take my gloves off so I can pry the metal away from the wall with my fingernails, but it still takes a good few tugs before it comes loose, showering me with dust. I wave my hand in front of my face to dissipate the motes as I stifle a cough.

That's the last thing I need to be doing right now.

When I'm certain I'm not going to dissolve into a coughing fit, I lean my head into the hole.

Just as dark as it always is, but enough light trickles in to confirm the ladder rungs are still welded into the metal walls of the shaft.

Here we go then.

I grab the grate in one hand and then use my other to help hoist my one foot onto the lip of the hole. Then I lift my other leg up and slowly turn around so I can back into the shaft.

My heart skips a beat as I miss the first ladder rung and I nearly drop the grate, but years of experience keeps me from losing my cool, and after a couple deep breaths, I find my footing. I take a few steps downward before I reach up and pull the grate back into place, sealing myself in.

Cracks of light flicker in through the metal, like flashes of lightning across my skin, and I breathe in deeply through my nose to steady myself.

You're okay. No one is going to hurt you.

He can't reach you here.

I tremble there in the dark for a few moments, my grip like iron against the ladder rungs.

Then I let out my breath and start descending further into the shadows, the light receding above me until it winks out.

Anane

The dungeons are a sea of red.

The torches on the walls illuminate the most gruesome scene I've ever witnessed, but I don't feel remorse, only power.

I did this. I cut those men down like they were nothing but dandelions, not strong enough to withstand an errant breeze.

A grin creeps onto my face, but it's not as big as the one Agent Eleven wears, and my skin prickles at the thought of it.

I told Father I didn't need him to complete this mission, but he insisted, and no one argues with the Master Assassin if they value their skin, so I let the psycho tag along. I let Silent Night and the others believe he was a nobody, while I put on a show.

I let Eleven think he was saving me, when I could've gotten myself out days ago if I wanted to.

Now he's standing in the middle of the dungeon grinning like an idiot, his boots stained crimson, as if all this destruction is his alone, as if this mission would've worked had I not been here to reel the Resistance in.

I've worked hard to get back into Father's good graces ever since Silent Night's escape, and I will not have this puny little man stealing all my glory. In fact, he would make a great example to the others beneath me that that is where they belong.

I clench my fist around my stolen sword and go to move toward him when I hear footsteps on the stairs.

The hair rises on my neck, and I slip back into my cell, retreating to the back corner where the shadows gather and the light can't quite reach.

Eleven is still standing in the middle of the room when Ruse walks in.

The man looks like he's entering a high society party instead of a massacre with his crisp suit and freshly polished shoes, neither of which are standard issue Resistance attire. A gold watch catches the light of the torches and I roll my eyes, wondering what dead millionaire he robbed to get it.

For a man who is supposed to be Father's most closely guarded secret, he sure likes to create a spectacle, though I wonder how much longer Father will keep his double agency under wraps. I wish I could stick around to see Silent Night's reaction, but my time here is over. Father needs me back home to start planning the real fun.

A smile ghosts across my face, and I step back into the light, joining Eleven and my uncle in the main area.

He gives me an appraising look. "Good to see *someone* retained their common sense while holed up here." He turns his near black eyes on Eleven and grimaces. "You're lucky it was me who came down those stairs, boy. This whole operation could've been ruined."

Eleven shrugs. "If it wasn't you, they would've met the same end as the rest. I would've handled it."

Ruse shoots out a hand, grabs Eleven by the chin with his fingernails, and yanks him forward before I can blink, so fast Eleven stumbles a bit.

I suppress the urge to grin.

"I will not have your arrogance put me on the Master Assassin's bad side, do you hear me?" Ruse seethes. "He might see potential in you, but all I see is a human suit around a rotting brain, and until you return to the Guild, you are under *my* thumb. You are being reckless if I say you are being reckless. You are nothing if I say you are. Do you understand me?"

Eleven nods, but I can see the defiance behind his eyes.

Ruse must see it too because he grips Eleven's face harder as he lets go, cutting into the skin.

Eleven wipes the blood away with the back of his hand, but otherwise acts as if nothing happened.

Asshole.

Ruse turns back to me. "Now if you two are done finger-painting like a pair of five-year-olds, the Master Assassin has one more task for you before you leave."

I raise an eyebrow. "What is it?"

Ruse smiles. "He'd like you to pay your sister one more visit, for old times' sake."

I frown. "What do you mean?"

Ruse pinches the bridge of his nose. "I suppose I'll have to spell it out for you then," he mutters. "He wants you to leave a blood trail to Silent Night's room and then vanish without a trace, so when she wakes up she'll know just how safe she really is, and that the Master Assassin spared her once again. She'll owe him, and we'll have sewn another seed of fear into her chest. Understood?"

I sheath my stolen sword. "I think I can manage that."

"Good," he says. "Take this one with you, and if he steps out of line, kill him, but do it quietly." He points at Eleven without looking at him, missing the vulgar gesture Eleven flips in his direction.

I ignore it and smile at Ruse. "It would be my pleasure."

"Then get going and don't disappoint me."

Trey

The tunnel always seems longer every time I descend into it, but eventually I reach the bottom, behind the wall of a mostly abandoned utility room. The lights are off, the door is shut, and the grate is at my feet, so I can't see anything. I wait in silence for the space of fifteen deep breaths as I strain to hear the presence of somebody inside.

Nothing stands out to me, not even the uneasy feeling that I might be walking into a trap, so I drop down onto my knees and push lightly against the grate from the bottom first. I don't want to knock it out on the tile floor.

It takes a moment, but I wedge it open, and then I push it forward lightly until the top end falls against my hands.

Bingo.

I set it against the outside wall and start maneuvering myself out of the hole, careful not to tear my cloak and leave evidence of my presence behind.

It's not easy, but I finally manage to pull myself free, emerging in a heap on the floor.

I lay there and breathe for a second, listening for company again, before I get to my feet and dust myself off. The room is just as I remember it, full of bent metal shelving units and ancient boxes of tissues and toilet paper. If I'm lucky, there will still be a plain grey uniform in the duffel bag under the far right shelf.

I walk over to it, using my memory to navigate the pitch black, and kneel down, brushing my hands lightly under the shelf. Nothing comes out to bite me, and I touch the familiar rough cloth of the bag a second later.

Thank the Guild.

I pull the bag out with both hands, lifting it so it doesn't scrape across the floor, and yank the button open quickly. The sound seems to reverberate in the small room, and I hold my breath, expecting the door to bang open any second, but no one comes. I'm still alone.

I take a deep breath and pull out the uniform, wondering if it will still fit me.

I roll my eyes at myself.

Assassins below, it hasn't been that long.

I smile at myself as I get changed, proving my common sense right when the uniform fits perfectly, just as it always has. I fold my cape up carefully with my other uniform and button them into the duffel bag before returning it to its place under the shelf.

I'll be back for you soon.

Standing alone in that plain grey uniform makes me feel like a new recruit again, lonely and afraid. Weak.

Well you're not the teenage girl you once were. You're making a difference now.

I hope so.

I whip my hair up into a bun as the final touch to my half-assed disguise. Any assassin worth their salt would recognize me as soon as they laid eyes on me, but I don't have the heart to not try at all. I need to get back to Kuen and Quinn, but more than that, I need to discover the truth. I need to know if I put my trust in the wrong person.

Again.

Anane

Silent Night's hallway is practically empty, and I wonder if it's more for their fear of her or her fear of them. In the Guild, no one dared to claim the rooms next to hers, not once she passed the rank of Agent Five. I always thought it was cowardice, but maybe it was intelligence. They would be easy kills if she really felt like it.

Still, if she had neighbours in this base, Eleven and I would've been caught by now.

Instead, we reach room 2413 without incident, just as Ruse promised us, and I almost laugh at how easy it was, at how easy it would be to slip inside and slit her throat while she sleeps.

Almost.

I know that looks can be deceiving, and this silent hall could just be another one of her tricks. She could be standing behind that door, gun in hand, ready to send us to our graves if we so much as knock.

Eleven doesn't seem to care and walks up to the door like he owns the place, his sword drawn. Ruse gave us back our weapons before we left the dungeon, and the weight of steel on my hip is a comfort I didn't know I needed.

My heart clenches when Eleven wraps his still-bloody hand around the doorknob.

He must notice the tension in the air because he turns to me and signs, "What?"

I relax my shoulders, not wanting him to think I'm afraid, and reply, "Just be careful."

He rolls his eyes and turns the doorknob slowly, before pushing the door into the room.

I'm surprised it isn't locked or barred from the inside, but Ruse did say Silent Night was growing complacent, getting comfortable. There's nothing more dangerous in this city than a sense of safety, and she should know that better than anyone.

Eleven slips into the room on silent feet and I follow, though I linger in the doorway while he stalks up to the bed.

Silent Night is sleeping soundly beneath the sheets with that boy from the dungeons curled around her back. I think I heard her call him Jax. A stupid name if you ask me.

She looks...almost peaceful lying there, as if the horrors of her past never happened, and for a moment, resentment flashes through me like fire.

But then I remember she's on the wrong side of this war and flash her a bitter smile.

Enjoy your so-called love while it lasts, while there's still air in your traitorous lungs. This charade will be over soon, and you'll be sorry you changed sides, sorry you walked away from everything Father gave you.

Across the room, Eleven is studying the pair intensely, as if he can't decide whether to join them or kill them. I give him a pointed look and hope he can feel my eyes burning into the back of his skull.

If he wakes them up…

I swear to God I'll let Silent Night kill him herself.

Finally, he steps away from the bed and turns back to me.

"What?" he signs again when he notices my expression.

"You're going to get us both killed," I sign back.

"You're no fun," he replies.

"Whatever, let's get out of here. We've done our job."

He gives Silent Night and Jax one last lingering look before following me back out into the hall, leaving the door ajar behind us.

I would like nothing more than to kill them both too, but it's not my job. Father specifically ordered us not to kill her, and I trust I'll be there when he finally does the deed. Besides, my next task promises to be even more satisfying. It's finally time to bring the original family traitor to justice.

Trey

The hallway outside the utility room is empty, and I take that as my last moment of luck for the day as I close the door behind me and set off. The bright lights of the base blind me for a few minutes after the darkness of the entry shaft, but I blink away my tears, knowing I need to be on high alert. My biggest asset will be my familiarity with the place, which will help me look like I belong.

My inner map is a bit dusty, but it shouldn't take too long to clear it off. I don't plan on being here long either. Just a quick look around, find some answers, and get out before I pay the price for trespassing, before my dear uncle notices I'm here and calls the dogs.

I smirk.

I'll kill a few before they bring me down. I may not be the youngest of the pack, but I'm not to be trifled with either. My age makes me wise where others are foolish and arrogant.

I reach the first intersection of halls and take a right, deeper into the base, not pausing for a second to think about it. There are a few more agents in this section, but I keep my head up and no one looks my way, at least not with questioning eyes.

A good start.

I'm not entirely sure where I'm going, but I have a feeling I'll know it when I see it, that something will just click and reveal everything to me.

It's a high hope, but I didn't leave the Warehouse with much of a plan, so it'll have to do.

I consider going to my room to see if there is any evidence there, but that will be a sure indication of my identity if anyone sees me, and I don't want to get blood on my expensive carpet, if it's even still there.

I feel a pang of sadness in my chest as I think of it, along with a sharp twinge of guilt.

Who cares if my things are gone if I'm still alive? I chastise myself. *Lives are at stake, and you're worried about a rug?*

It's not important, and yet, there's a part of me that refutes that.

The little things are allowed to bother you no matter what because once upon a time they mattered, more than anything.

That rug was the first impractical thing I ever bought for myself, and the freedom I felt when I got it was unparalleled. It might be gone, like so many other things in my life, but it will always mean something more to me than it will ever mean to someone else.

I take a deep breath to clear out my emotions, closing my eyes for a split second, and then refocus on the task at hand. My feet have carried me to the main hub of the Barn, a massive atrium with eight halls branching off it like spokes of a wheel and multiple floors stacked above me.

The area is packed with people of all ages dressed in different shades of grey, a familiar sight, but the energy in the room is off. Tainted. It feels as though everyone is holding their breath, as if everyone is waiting for an axe to drop. The hairs on my arm stand on end as I realize what this reminds me of.

This is exactly what it felt like at the Guild—a constant, almost tangible fear hanging in the air, the threat of the Charger a never-ending reality.

It is in that moment that I know the Resistance East has been lost.

I don't have to interrogate an agent. I don't have to torture it out of Avery. I don't need to see another assassin face I recognize. I can feel the truth in my bones and in the memories that rise to the surface of my skin. I can feel it in the shiver that works its way down my spine as the unease of the room filters into me.

The assassins are here.

And then, in the corner of my eye, I see something even worse. I see something that confirms what I already know.

Across the room, walking side by side with Avery Norin, is Sephtis Aeron.

The Master Assassin is here.

Anane

Ruse lets Eleven and I out through a door hidden in the back of a janitor's closet. It's so well disguised I almost thought he was looking for a quiet place to slit our throats, until the door slid out of the wall as if materializing from thin air.

The tunnel beyond is dark, but even though it could possess countless unknown dangers, I feel a sense of calm rush through me at the sight. Freedom awaits at the other end. Despite the plan being to escape all along, there was still a part of me that feared being left behind, a doubt that I will always carry with me.

I know my father is not a decent man. Yet, he holds a power over me and others that I can't describe or even begin to imagine for myself. There was always a chance he would leave me behind, that he would leave me to rot in that dungeon or that Ruse would, but here I am.

Alive to kill another day.

I smirk.

Life is truly a cruel adventure.

"Now remember," Ruse says, "Trey has gone to investigate the Barn. It is crucial that you find her before she discovers our secret and reports back to Jenson. The Charger doesn't care what you do to her, as long as you bring her to him alive. I'm told he has the 'most gruesome' plan in mind for her, so I'm sure he will be very disappointed if someone gets trigger-happy. Understood?"

He sets us both in his severe black gaze, and we nod, though not out of fear. I've been living under my father's death glare for twenty-seven years, and Ruse has nothing on the terror that can bring.

"You best be on your way then," Ruse says. "And remember, if you find yourselves back in those dungeons, I won't be helping you. My deal is done until the Charger calls on me again."

"We won't forget your kindness," Eleven replies.

I know it's poor judgment, but I crack a small smile at that one. I have a few choice words for my dear uncle too, though I don't dare voice them. Having my father on my back all the time is bad enough. I don't need any more enemies.

"Come on, Agent," I say before Ruse can strike him again. "The Charger doesn't like to be kept waiting."

Eleven glares at me but does as he's told, unsheathing his sword as he steps in front of me and into the tunnel without looking back.

"Keep an eye on that one," Ruse warns me.

"I have it covered," I reply.

"I hope so," he says. "I'd hate to lose another nephew." He grins at me, and I take that as my sign to leave.

Out of all the assassins in this world, I'm certainly not going to let Eleven be the death of me. I'm not ranked

Agent Two for nothing, and if there's one thing being the Charger's son has taught me, it's how to survive.

Besides, everyone in the Guild knows the Master's children are off limits now. The only person allowed to kill the Aeron children is the Master himself, and Father hasn't grown tired of me yet.

I hope to live long enough to see the Resistance crumble, to gain a place of power in the new Haven City that will emerge from the ashes, but I'll take whatever victory I can get, even if it means just living one more day, one day at a time.

Life may be a cruel adventure, but each sunrise is a new opportunity for greatness, and I intend to be remembered.

Trey

My eyes stay on Sephtis for a split second before my feet take over and start carrying me in the opposite direction as fast as they can go without raising suspicion.

I never would've come inside if I knew he was here, but there's nothing I can do about it now. Whatever happens, I need to warn the Warehouse before he finds me. Failure is not an option because if I don't tell them what I know, the Resistance will lose this war, and that is not a reality I want to live in.

Death is a sweeter melody than demise when your future is not the only one on the line.

The fear hanging in the air turns into a thick, cloying fog as I leave the atrium behind, every inch of my mind screaming that it's too late.

He's seen you.

It's over.

I ignore it all and keep moving.

Failure is not *an option.*

Only when I am several hallways away do I slow my pace and take a few deep breaths. The crowds have thinned out some, but that almost makes me more anxious, like I'm a deer in an open field just begging to be shot.

Just breathe, I tell myself. *Freaking out is not going to help anyone.*

I take a couple shuddering breaths that slowly even out, and I clench my fists until my hands stop shaking. No one has taken a stab at me yet, so I'm still here, still alive.

I can do this.

Now, what's the plan?

Instinctually, I want to return to the utility room, don my cape again, and disappear into the storm, but I know deep down that it's not meant to be. The Warehouse is several kilometres away, and too much could go wrong in the time it would take me to get back.

No, I need to send my message now, and there's only one way to do it.

• • •

My room is exactly how I left it. Purple curtains hang intact around my four-poster bed, my expensive rug lies across the hardwood at the foot of the bed, and my closet stands open, revealing a row of blood red capes.

I shut the door behind me, slide the ten bolts across, and flick the switch on my bedside lamp.

An orange glow fills the space, and I take a moment to absorb my surroundings. It feels so...surreal standing here again, after everything. It feels liberating, and yet, bittersweet, like I will never stand here again.

I shake off that feeling and walk around my bed. Then I use all my strength to push the bed across the floor until it's in front of the door. It won't last forever, but it'll buy me time.

I roll my shoulders and then walk over to my desk, where a phone sits in a receiver against the wall, one of the few direct lines to the Warehouse. I pray that it hasn't been disconnected as I pick it up and hit a random button.

The phone admits a beep, and my heart skips a beat. *Thank God.*

I rifle in the top drawer of my desk for the phone number and punch it in without another thought. With the Master Assassin lurking around, I don't have time to spare. He could walk through the door any second now, so I have to make this count.

The phone rings for what feels like forever, and then there's a soft click on the other end followed by a voice. "You have reached 803-931-25807, how may I direct your call today?"

It's the standard, anonymous greeting, and I struggle to remember the correct response.

"Hello?" the person says.

"Sorry," I stammer. "Um... I would like to place an order for a medium pizza, hold the pepperoni."

"This is the Warehouse," the person replies. "Can I ask who is calling?"

I breathe a sigh of relief. "Yes, this is Trey Ballinger, Avery's Second, typically based out of the Barn, but I've been at the Warehouse for the past little while."

"What is the password, Trey?"

"The fight isn't over until Haven City is dust beneath our boots and there is no one left to save."

"Long live the Resistance," he replies. "What can I do for you today?"

"I have a message to relay," I tell him. "It's very important that you write it out word for word and deliver it to Jenson immediately."

"Of course," he replies. "I am ready when you are."

"Jenson," I begin, "I have reached the Barn and done some preliminary observations." I pause. "It seems it is worse than I feared. My suspicions were right and then some."

I take a deep breath.

"I didn't want to consider it, didn't want to believe it, but it is nothing but the truth. The Resistance East has been compromised. It's crawling with assassins. I believe they've been hiding out here since the *fall* of the Guild."

The man on the other end doesn't react to my words, but I can imagine the dismay on his face, the ache in his chest at the news.

"I hope this message reaches you before it's too late," I go on. "The Warehouse is in grave danger. Don't let Anane escape."

The last sentence is almost an afterthought, but I know that after all the advantages we've just lost, we can't afford to lose him, not that Sephtis would care too much if he did.

I'm about to sign off my message when I hear a knock on the door.

My blood runs cold.

He's found me.

"Trey, are you still there?"

"Yes," I reply, my voice barely above a whisper.

The rest of my message fizzles out of my head as I hear the door knob rattle and then someone trying to shove the door open.

Shit.

I'm not going to make it back to the Warehouse now.

"Trey," the voice on the other end of the line says, "is that the end of your message?"

"Um, no," I reply, my hands shaking as the door continues to rattle. "The rest goes like this."

Tears start falling down my face silently as I lie through my teeth, hoping to spare Quinn and Kuen the pain of the truth. I'm never going to see them again.

"I'm sending this message back to you, and then I'm going in. If you don't hear from me within a day or so, I give you the right to assume the worst. Do not, under any circumstances, round up a search party. I'm not worth the lives you will lose. Trey."

I take a shuddering breath as someone in the hall starts yelling at me to come out.

"We know you're in there!"

"Come out if you know what's good for you!"

"The Charger wants to have some words…"

"P.S.," I add. "If this is how it ends, tell Kuen and Quinn I am sorry, and I love them. Stay strong, guys. End message."

The voices outside grow louder, but I focus on the one on the line.

"I've got it all down," he says. "I will take it to Jenson as soon as we're done."

"Good," I say. "Long live the Resistance."
Then I hang up the phone.

ONE FEARFUL CHOICE

Haven City, 08/2110

Natalie

I wake up screaming, my nightgown clinging to my back, my brothers' faces fading even as I try desperately to hold onto them.

I watch them die in my nightmares every night. I lose them again and again, and yet, some part of me is grateful for it because if I can still dream about them, it means I haven't forgotten what they look like. It means they're still with me.

I let out a deep, shuddering breath as the dream finally lets me go, and I open my eyes, the gruesome events already gone from my memory.

It's amazing how quickly a dream can disappear, the only sign of its presence the lingering anxiety in your chest and the beating of your heart.

The room around me is dark and dingy, just as it always is, and not for the first time, I long for my childhood bedroom. I long for the gossamer curtains around the bed and the ability to jump up and throw the drapes out from the window to let in the morning light.

I hardly ever see the sun now. Some days I worry that I've forgotten what it feels like, but I guess I have bigger problems than that, like the fact that I haven't slept soundly in almost two months.

Even now, the thought of getting out of bed is almost more than I can bear.

What's the point?

Just to go through the motions of a normal day once again? Just to come back here tonight and relive their deaths for the hundredth time?

I play this game with myself every morning, but the result is always the same. I throw off my blankets, roll into a sitting position, and hop out of bed, wincing as my bare feet hit the cold concrete floor.

The result is always the same because the alternative would be a lecture from my father, and that is a conversation I would like to avoid at all costs. I'm already dirt beneath his shoes; I don't need to shoulder any more of his disappointment.

Besides, the less I see of him, the better. The less I see of him, the less likely I am to do something stupid and get myself killed.

I want him dead, but not as much as I want to live, and I am not strong enough to accomplish both yet.

I shuffle over to my closet and discard my nightgown in favour of another dull grey uniform. Another thing I miss about my old house is the colour I had in my wardrobe. What I wouldn't give for some pink or purple, a little variety to my days.

Next stop is my en suite bathroom, to attempt to cover up the heavy, purple bags beneath my eyes and to coax some colour back into my cheeks. Some days, I can almost convince myself there's nothing wrong with me, at least while looking in a mirror, but it gets harder every day to hide the truth.

Jenson can sense there's something off, but he has no idea what my father did, who my father truly is. Jenson still worships the ground he walks on, would let him get away with murder, and I… I can't bring myself to shatter his reality.

I can't bring myself to betray my father, even after everything he's done.

Jesper

There is a weight to the air as I look across the city, and I know Sephtis is close. I'm crouched on the edge of an empty factory, three streets away from the Warehouse, the heat of the summer sun beating down on me.

I wipe my brow.

There is always a certain risk to wearing black, and yet, I can't get away from it, not when I'm forced to wear those infernal grey uniforms any other time, not when black reminds me of home and a simpler life.

What I wouldn't give some days to bring it all back...

What I wouldn't have given back then for it to all burn sooner...

"Either you're ignoring me," a voice drawls behind me, "or you've let yourself get rusty."

I roll my eyes and stand up to my full height, stretching my arms above me before turning to face my brother.

"I was merely seeing how long you would wait," I reply with a smile.

He nods. "I see."

"You look good, Sef," I say, taking in his strong frame and the lack of grey in his dark hair.

He flinches at the name but lets it slide, lets the memories run through him before composing himself into the stone statue I've come to know over the past twenty years.

I like to remind him now and again of who he was, who he will always be to me.

"You look like you could use a new mission," he replies, straight to the point as per usual.

I sigh and shove my hands in my pocket. "Who am I letting out of the dungeon this time? It better not be that sorry excuse of a son you have."

Sephtis grins. "Which one?"

I laugh. "Touché. Seriously though, what do you need me to do?"

His smile grows wider. "It is time, my dear Ruse, to blow your cover and exterminate the rodent problem at the Warehouse. There are too many greycoats there for my liking, and I'm quite close to bringing Silent Night back to my side, but I need her tired and broken first."

I raise an eyebrow. "You really think she'll come back?"

"Not of her own free will," Sephtis replies, "but I am done playing nice. Vyrin is working on something...special for her."

A chill settles into my bones. As much as the girl enrages me to no end, I hate to imagine what Sephtis is going to do to her. I just hope he's considered the consequences.

"So I'm blowing my cover," I prompt, bringing us back on track. "What exactly will that entail?"

He rolls his shoulders before answering, as if this is a casual conversation, as if we're not talking about revealing my double agency after nineteen years.

"Well, first I will need you to let me into the base tonight with Trey, and then after that, you'll call on your undercover assassins to start an uprising. While they're busy killing the rabble, I want you to get me Jenson."

Ah.

I give him a look. "Still salty that Silent Night didn't hand him over?"

He glares at me, but I don't look away. "She made the wrong choice, I can promise you that, and once she sees the consequences of her actions, it will eat away at her for the rest of her life. You don't deny me what I want without risking your own sanity."

I nod. It was a lesson I learned the hard way several times over the years, and yet, I still can't help but stoke a small fire of defiance.

"It just goes to show that if you want something done right, you have to do it yourself," he goes on.

"Then why are you getting me to do it?"

"Because I have more important things to do, Jesper," he snaps, "and I trust that you will get the job done or die trying."

I roll my eyes. "Calm down there, big brother. We don't need you having a heart attack before you've completed your life's work. Jes can get it done, don't worry."

He gives me an unamused look. "Many more quips like that, *brother*, and I *will* do it myself, after burying you in a shallow, unmarked grave that I will never visit."

I grin. "I love you too; now tell me all the details of your gruesome plan before it gets dark. I need to know what I'm working with."

He sighs. "You always were a strange one."

And he always had a soft spot for me, though I wonder how much longer that lenience will last. I wonder if he would mourn me if I passed or if his heart has shrivelled up so much that I'll get merely a passing thought before he moves on to the next scheme.

I wonder if he cares enough to avenge me.

Natalie

The base seems extra loud today as I go to my various lectures, my mind in a haze. I discover after my third that although I took my notebook and pen out, I left the pages completely blank and don't remember a word of what the professor said. It's sad, but I can't really bring myself to care as I head to the cafeteria for lunch.

There's a slim chance I'll ever amount to anything anyway, so why aim for greatness?

I'll just do my best to finish my classes and then rot in my father's shadow for the next twenty years while I pretend to like my lot in life, while I wait for him and my uncles to kill us all, or for the courage to do it first.

My stomach heaves, and I set down my spoon, leaning away from the scented steam rising off my vegetable soup.

Not for the first time, I wonder how it feels to kill someone.

Is there a rush of adrenaline or a feeling like ice running down your back?

Does your mind run the scene on repeat until you never want to sleep again?

Do you ever forgive yourself?

But worse is the fear that I won't feel anything, that I would kill him without remorse and damn the consequences. I'm afraid that in killing him, I'll lose a piece of myself.

I try to tell myself that it's worth the risk, but at the end of the day, he's still my father. He raised me. He saved me from nightmares when I was small. He bandaged my scraped knees and bought me teddy bears.

I want to believe that it couldn't all have been lies, but it's hard to tell anymore.

It's hard to ignore the voice in my head that whispers he isn't the man he used to be, if he ever was.

Jesper

Words could not have prepared me for the state my once proud niece is in. Sephtis drags her in through the tunnel and deposits her in a heap on the tile floor of the utility closet. Her cape is torn to shreds, her face is almost unrecognizable, and the rest of her...

Assassins below.

I'd seen a lot of terrible things in my life, most when I was too young to comprehend their significance, but this... This might top the list.

I gesture to her unconscious body as I eye my brother. "Your handiwork, I presume?"

He shakes his head. "Again, I have more important things to do. No, this was Anane, under my guidance, of course. The two have a rivalry, much different than him and Quinn, but almost better."

I give him a look. "Meaning?"

He scowls. "Meaning that Anane was better suited to torturing her than I was, and I dare say he performed beyond my expectations. I dare say Trey regrets not killing him when she had the chance." His scowl morphs into a grin, and I force myself to echo it.

"What will you do with her now?" I ask.

"Leave her here to die or be rescued, if Silent Night and her friends are clever enough. Even still, she doesn't have much time left. I predict that they'll be watching her die in a week or so, if they find her in time."

"Well, I guess I'll leave you to it then. See you on the other side, Sef."

He nods. "Don't disappoint me."

Natalie

As I'm walking back from a lonely dinner in the cafeteria, I can feel a shift in the air, like someone is pulling a bowstring taut and aiming it straight at me. The hallways are almost empty, which is unusual for this hour, and now that I think about it, the cafeteria was hardly crowded either.

Something is up.

It's been three days since the base was put into lockdown, three days since Trey was captured by the assassins, since my father helped Anane and his lackey escape. Everyone has been waiting for the assassins to attack, but they don't realize that the assassins are already here.

And they're about to make their move.

I decide then and there that I am done sitting on the sidelines, I'm done being nothing more than a pretty little doll. My father has used my talents to his own ends for years, but he made a mistake in doing so because he gave me an edge. I have become the Resistance's best chance of surviving this inevitable attack, and I won't let it go to waste.

I run scenarios through my mind as I stand in the middle of the hall, trying to figure out my father's plan, where he will strike first. I need to be there to stop him. Even if I can't kill him, I can still make a difference.

My mind is still racing when I hear a gunshot go off in the distance.

Shit.

It's already happening.

I have to get out of the open.

I duck into the nearest room and shut the door, sliding the lock across. I can still hear gunfire echoing through the base and then the PA system screeches to life, sending a shiver through my bones.

"All agents to their posts," Jenson's voice calls out, trying desperately to be heard over the static. "There has been a security breach. I repeat, everyone to arms. We are under attack. I repeat—"

My blood runs cold as his voice cuts off and everything clicks into place.

My father is after Jenson.

And right now, I'm the only one who can save him.

I take a deep breath to steady myself and look around the room for a weapon. Nothing jumps out at me, but it's a lecture room and I know a few inside tricks.

I walk over to the professor's desk and slide my hands along the underside of it until I find a metal switch. I flick it over, and after a few clicks and groans, a secret drawer pops open, revealing a shiny, silver pistol and six cartridges.

I load the gun with shaking hands and then click the drawer shut again.

Six chances to get this right, I muse, but I know that one missed shot will spell my demise, especially when it comes to my father.

Still, I have to try.

I'm coming for you, Jenson, I promise. Just hold on.

Jesper

My skin is alight with nerves as I walk down the hall towards the control room. Gunfire rattles the walls all around me as my men tear off their disguises and reveal the monsters underneath, but the pressure is on me.

This will all be for nothing if I can't kill Jenson, if I can't complete the simple task Sephtis gave me. I need to get to him before he locks himself in the safe room, because the only one with a code is him and Vyrin, and Vyrin will not be coming over here to save my ass.

I pick up the pace, taking halls I know should be abandoned at this time of day—not that it matters too much if someone sees me. Until Jenson is dead, the Resistance will still believe I'm on their side, and my men know that if they shoot me, Sephtis will have their skin.

When I reach the control room, the door is locked, and I pound on it frantically.

"It's Ross, Jenson!" I call out, putting some desperation in my voice. "I just used my last bullet. You have to let me in!"

"What's the password?" a voice calls from within.

I smile. What a sad attempt at security. "The fight isn't over until Haven City is dust beneath our boots," I reply, "and there is no one left to save."

No one answers from within, but I hear a series of clicks and bangs as Jenson unbars the door and swings it open, greeting me with a smile.

"Oh thank God you're still alive," he says as he ushers me in and reholsters his pistol. "I don't know how the assassin got in but we have to—"

He stops mid-sentence as I raise my own gun and press the cold metal into his forehead.

"Nicholas," he says, a note of fear in his voice, "what are you doing?"

"Something I should've done years ago," I reply. "Now get on the ground where you belong."

I keep the gun aimed at his head as I kick his legs out from underneath him. He hits the ground hard, curses flying, and reaches for his gun, but I step on his other wrist and he screams, rolling towards that side. I lean down and strike him across the face with my gun. Then I take his gun and throw it across the room before he can recover.

He spits out blood, breathing heavily through the pain, and I watch him in disgust.

"You never were strong enough for greatness, Jenson," I tell him, "and now, you'll never get the chance to prove me wrong."

"Always...so arrogant," Jenson chokes out. "Perhaps...you should've made sure...I was alone...before...revealing your secrets."

Shit.

I hit the ground as a gunshot rings out behind me.

Natalie

My father is already there when I reach the control room, but it seems I wasn't the only one who predicted the assassins' intentions. There are five Resistance agents facing off with him when I enter the hall, and Jenson is nowhere in sight, though I have a feeling he's inside the control room, tied up or otherwise incapacitated.

I crouch in a doorway a little ways down from the control room and watch the fight unfold. It kills me to wait in silence while these people die, but I've already used five of my bullets to get this far, and I have to make the last one count.

Three of the agents are shot in the head, joining the dead quickly, but my father takes his time with the other two, taunting them and tearing them apart slowly before slitting one's throat and suffocating the other to death.

I choke back the bile that rises to the back of my throat at the sight.

There's so much blood.

And you just sat there and let it happen.

I tell myself there was nothing I could do, but the guilt is a living thing, like a snake wrapping itself around my neck.

Father is wiping his hands on his pants when Jenson stumbles out of the control room, a knife in hand.

I raise my gun to offer him support, but my father is already moving. He disarms Jenson before I can aim properly and then shoves Jenson to his knees in front of him, his gun to Jenson's head. Jenson lets out a scream as his knees hit the concrete.

Shit.

I need to get closer, but he'll hear me as soon as I move, I know it.

What I wouldn't give right now for a distraction…

And then, like some kind of miracle, a group of agents round the corner, and my heart drops into my toes as I recognize one of them as Quinn.

Jesper

I'm just about to finish Jenson off when a group of agents come running into the hall, the three of them skidding to a stop when they see me.

"You!" one of them spits out, and I realize with glee that it is Ajax Forrester, which means…

Ah yes, there's Silent Night behind him, that fire still present behind her eyes. If only she knew what Sephtis has planned for her.

"So we meet again, Ross," she says, not shying away from my gaze, "and my, what an interesting turn of events."

I smile. "Call me Ruse. I'm sure you've heard of me, Silent Night."

There is no greater joy than watching the pain and disbelief ripple through her.

"You're lying," she says. "Ruse is just—"

"A legend?" I offer with a laugh. "Dear girl, I thought you of all people would know better than that. Ruse became a legend because that's what Sephtis wanted all of you to believe. He's always pulling the strings."

"And you're totally okay with being a puppet?" she counters. "Wait…" she adds, a hint of fear creeping into her voice. "How do you know the Charger's name?"

Oh, this is too much fun.

"Aside from the fact that Jenson told me a few days ago?"

"Yes, aside from that," she replies, waving a hand. "You say it as though you're comfortable with it."

I shrug and say, "Well, brothers should be comfortable saying each other's names, don't you think?"

Her eyes widen in shock, and I grin. "Surprise! I bet you thought the revelations were over. Who would've thought? Nicholas Ross, the third Aeron brother? But it is nothing but the truth. Who else would Sephtis charge with such a task? I am paramount to his success."

Something dawns in her eyes. "It was you," she says. "You were the one who told Anane where my room was."

I smile. "Good, you're starting to catch on."

"But why?" she asks. "Why bother?"

I shrug again. "Why not? It was fun, toying with you, trying to break you. This entire organization has been nothing but a game for years, and you, my dear Jenson, were but a willing pawn."

I look down at Jenson and pat him on the head, grinning as he tries to jerk away, only to have my dagger jab into his side.

A small gasp escapes him.

I stroke his cheek. "Shhh…" I tell him. "It'll all be over soon."

"Don't touch me, you traitorous wretch," he spits.

Again, he tries to pull away.

Again, my dagger meets his flesh.

I click my tongue. "Touchy."

"Let him go," Silent Night says, as if asking politely will get her what she wants.

"Or what?" I counter. "Are you going to continue your bloody tirade and kill another uncle?"

The sight of her blood draining out of her face is a sweet victory.

"What did you just say?"

I smile.

Checkmate.

"You heard me," I reply. "You just don't want to believe it."

"Stop with the games!" she snaps. "Tell us why you're really here."

"I'm here to tear the Resistance apart from the inside out," I fire back, "to kill Jenson, and eradicate any hope of ever beating the Guild. You will all lose. Don't you see? You never had a chance. Avery was a lie. I was a lie. A third of the Agents here are actually mine. Whatever good you thought you accomplished, well, it was all a ruse."

I laugh at my own joke, but Silent Night is less than amused.

She pulls out her gun and aims it at me.

"Step away from Jenson."

Natalie

My heart skips a beat when Quinn takes out her gun and points it at my father. I've been moving closer to the group ever since they showed up, using their conversation to mask my steps as I walk along the wall from doorway to doorway.

My father shakes his head. "Put that away, or he'll be dead before you can pull the trigger."

To my surprise, Quinn listens to him, though I can tell from the look on her face that she would rather wring his neck.

Just a few more feet.

"He misses you, you know," my father says.

Quinn raises an eyebrow. "Who?"

"Your father."

"He's not my father," Quinn snaps, "and if you think playing at that is going to bring me over to your side… You're more stupid than I thought."

I smile.

I wish I had the guts to say that to him.

"He wants you to come home," my father goes on, as if Quinn had said nothing.

"This is my home," she spits at him, "and I don't give a damn what he wants."

I can imagine my father smiling at her as he says, "Good to know that Silent Night still has her fire."

"That is not my name!"

"Leave her alone!" Jax growls.

I wince at their tones, sensing that this confrontation is about to reach its violent crescendo. I'm almost in position now.

"And what will you do, Forrester, that she can't?" my father replies. "You're pathetic, the both of you. All this talk of love…" He turns back to Quinn. "Yet, Sephtis is willing to forget all that, if you return."

I step away from the wall and start walking towards my father, my gun raised in shaking hands.

"I'm not going back to his enslavement," Quinn snaps, "so you can save your breath."

Almost there.

My father shrugs and says, "It was worth a try." Then he takes a deep breath. "Well, chatting was fun, but I have a job to do. Jenson? Shall we?" He slings one arm around Jenson's throat and presses the barrel of his gun harder into Jenson's skull.

I aim my gun at the back of his head.

His finger tightens on the trigger.

My vision sharpens, and I pull the trigger first.

Not this time, Father.

The shot goes off with a bang that echoes throughout the hall, and for a moment, it's like time stands still. The smell of gunpowder invades my nostrils.

Then my father slumps over to the ground, Jenson falling away from him, and it hits me, what I've done.

I killed him.

I killed my father.

My hands start shaking uncontrollably as I stare at his body, lying there unmoving on the floor.

What have I done?

"Natalie?" a voice says.

I look over to see Quinn staring at me, concern and a hint of fear in her eyes.

"You... You don't understand," I gasp, all my fear and anger spilling out at once after being bottled up since I could talk. "I h-had to. You were right, Assassin, I do care. And he..." Tears start streaming down my face as I think of my brothers again, as I remember what I have to look forward to if I manage to fall asleep tonight.

"He killed them all!"

The pain is almost too much to bear, and I sink to the floor, a couple feet away from the man who used to be my father, once upon a time.

• • •

We're all monsters.

The line has been playing in my head ever since my conversation with Quinn because of how incredibly true it is. Nobody on this earth is free of sin, but it's not about what happened in the past; it's about what we do in the here and now and I am no longer going to sit in the shadows watching the world die.

I want to fight. I want to show the world what I'm capable of. I want to help the Resistance win. Not for me, not for my brothers, but for all the people out there who are helpless, like me. For all the people who don't have the strength to fight.

We're all monsters, and sometimes, it takes a monster to win a war.

ONE FATAL MISTAKE

Haven City, 11/2104

Kuen

There are many things about death that you can learn to forget, to forgive: the splashes of blood all over your clothes and skin, the screams of your victims, and the echoes of the gunshots hanging in the air. You can even learn to forget how it makes you feel, to become numb to all the pain and suffering, but one thing you can't chase is the smell.

The sickly scent of iron and other, unpleasant bodily fluids invades my nostrils as I step foot in the room. I gag on the weight of it as it clogs my throat and am quick to pull the collar of my shirt up over my nose to give me some relief.

Guild, how long has this body been here?

Weeks, I imagine, judging from the smell alone.

It doesn't take me long to find the murder scene, as if the blood spatter on the far wall isn't enough to go by. The body is slumped on the floor beside the bed, looking as if it slid down the wall after being shot point blank in the head. In fact, I can see the bullet itself embedded in the drywall.

Poor unlucky bastard.

There's not much left of the body, but I don't see other wounds or any signs of a struggle in the room. The bed is still perfectly made, the lamp on the nightstand still upright, though covered in a layer of dust.

What happened here?

More importantly, why does Sephtis care?

It's just another dead body in the hundreds we create each year. Why does it matter, and why did he send me to look into it?

I heave a sigh of frustration and set about scouring the rest of the room and house for clues when I hear a floorboard creak somewhere below me.

I freeze and listen intently for further movement, but the house remains silent, and that is when I realize why I am here.

Sephtis sent someone to kill me.

I grin.

The old man never learns.

I'm not giving up the title of Agent One for anyone or anything, and I'm certainly not going to fall for any of his traps.

I inch my way behind the door of the room, leaving it fully open, and draw my gun. I have a full six shots left, but I intend to walk away from this encounter only one bullet lighter.

The other assassin's approach up the stairs is almost perfect, but I can still hear the slight sound of their boots touching and leaving the wood of each step, and then the softest of footfalls as they continue down the hall towards me.

One of my biggest advantages in the Guild is my acute hearing. I don't know if I inherited it from my long-dead mother, or the Master Assassin himself, but it's saved my life quite a few times, and it drives the other assassins crazy with jealousy.

The footsteps stop as the assassin hesitates in front of the open doorway, and I slow my breathing as I watch him through the crack between the door and the jam.

Just a few more steps.

Come on. I know you want to.

Finally, the man squares his shoulders, raises his own gun, and steps into the room.

That's when I strike.

He gets his first leg inside and is about to follow through with the second when I kick the door towards him with all my might, sending him flying back into the hall.

A couple shots go off as the shock of the moment poisons his mind, and I smile.

Only four bullets left.

I enter the hall and tackle him back to the floor before he can fully get to his feet.

A third shot goes off, but it misses me by a mile, and I disarm him before he can try another, sending his pistol skidding across the hardwood floor.

He fights me off as I toy with him, even landing a couple good punches to the face, but it was clear from the start that I had the upper hand. This kid is scrawnier than an orphan on the streets and barely any taller, nothing compared to my hulking height.

When he tries to roll me, I throw my head back and laugh.

"Is that the best you got?" I ask him. "Damn, the Charger really is running out of worthy adversaries."

My hands have left him for a second, along with most of my body weight, and he grins, thinking he's found an opening, not realizing I did it intentionally.

He reaches for something in his side pocket and rears up as he drives a four-inch-long knife into my chest.

At least he tries to.

Fear solidifies in his eyes as the blade pierces my shirt but then glances off the metal armour underneath.

"What—"

The rest of his sentence is drowned out by my gunshot as I bury a bullet in his head.

Sephtis

When my son flings open the door to my office and deposits a bloody skull on my desk, there are a few emotions I can choose from—anger, disappointment, disgust—but I go for the one that will annoy him the most, my face settling on cool disinterest as I say, "And what do we have here?"

He gives me a look that is borderline traitorous, a glint to his blue eyes that shows his heritage more than his appearance ever will, but like his father, he schools his features into indifference and says, "I brought you a present. Poor bastard tried to kill me today during my mission. I figured it was only right for me to put him out of his misery."

I swallow back my own annoyance.

I taught him too well.

My eyes flick to the shelf on the far wall as I reply, "I'll add him to my collection." I squint at the head. "It is a he, isn't it?"

He nods. "Was, but you already knew that."

I tilt my head and lean back in my chair. "I'm not sure what you mean?"

He shrugs. "Oh, we don't have to get into it. I just thought I'd let you know that I'm not an idiot, in case you forgot."

"I see," I reply, fighting to keep my voice in check. His insolence has only grown over the years, but he has an intimate understanding of how far he can push me before I break. It's a dangerous thing, his understanding, and I don't like it one bit. The longer he survives, the more dangerous he becomes, but the longer he survives, the harder he is to kill.

He's held the title of Agent One for seven years now, longer than anyone in the history of the ranking system, and no one I've sent after him has gotten even close to knocking him off his pedestal.

I'm going to need more space on my shelf.

"Anyway," he goes on, "that's all I wanted to talk about. Is there any news, or am I free to go?"

"There is one thing," I answer, as I toy with a ring on my left hand. "There is going to be an execution tonight, if your sister manages to bring the traitor in."

He blinks. "You made Quinn the executioner? She's, what, ten years old?"

"Twelve," I correct him, "and perfectly capable of filling the position. Have you heard that people have started calling her Silent Night?"

I beam at the thought and hope my pride makes him seethe with rage. I haven't yet tried to kill my youngest daughter, not directly anyway.

"Not a bad name," he replies.

I nod. "I think it will serve her well. In any case, I expect you to be at the execution tonight, and I expect you to keep your sister alive, no matter the circumstance."

He rolls his eyes. "Oh, so she's strong enough to be the executioner but not strong enough to survive the massacre?"

I swipe the severed head off my desk, letting it drop onto his boots. "I didn't ask you to question me; I gave you an order. Your sister is to walk out of there unharmed, or the next execution will be your own. Do you understand me?"

He doesn't acknowledge the skull at his feet as he says, "It will be done."

I cross my arms. "Good. Now get out of my sight; I have work to do."

He gives me a mock bow and then flips me the middle finger as he leaves the room, ducking the knife that I throw at his retreating back.

Yes, I taught him much too well indeed.

Kuen

Adrenaline rushes through me as I leave my father's office behind. There's nothing quite like seeing how far you can push a monster before it snaps. Each step I take these days is balanced on the edge of a precipice, but I can't bring myself to care. Flirting with death is the only thing that keeps life interesting.

Still, I'm troubled by his words.

Quinn must be the youngest executioner in history, and it's going to be a bitch to keep her alive, not to mention doing it in a way that doesn't show my hand so the other assassins don't think I'm babying her. If I kill her social standing, she's as good as dead. It won't be long before everyone comes to test her weakness, and try as I might, I won't be able to save her from all of them.

Still, I promised Trey I'd protect her.

I close my eyes then as I try to picture Trey's face: her smile at my terrible jokes, the fire in her eyes when she spoke of our father, the warmth in them when she told me I wasn't a monster, time and time again.

She's twenty-three years old now, and I haven't seen her in seven years. Anything could've happened since then, but something tells me she's thriving, that she's fighting against our father's reign, and that one day, she's going to be a hero. Unlike me. My darkness is a lonely path that I will tread until I die, but if I can keep Trey's promise, it will be enough.

• • •

That night, I'm leaning against the wall of the Grand Cavern, dressed to the nines in steel, when Hai saunters over with the usual unhinged grin on his face.

"Hey," he says, "I hear there's going to be a big show tonight. Everybody's whispering about a traitor."

I nod. "The Charger told me."

He frowns. "How come he let you in on the secret?"

I shrug. "Because I'm Agent One? How should I know? He does what he likes. Don't act like it's an advantage; it's probably part of some elaborate scheme to get me killed."

He rolls his eyes and leans up against the wall beside me. "He doesn't want to kill you."

"No, he doesn't want to kill me *himself*, but he still wants me dead. It aggravates him to no end that I'm still standing."

"I hear he's appointed a new executioner," Hai says, ignoring my reply. He crosses his arms. "I wonder who the lucky bastard is."

I grin. "Still bitter that he won't let it be you?"

He scowls. "No one else belongs in that role more than me."

"There would be no one left to execute if you had that role," I counter. "Face it, Hai. The Charger needs someone with a little more…control. If you had what it takes, he'd have given it to you already."

"Oh, I suppose it's you then, isn't it?" he sneers. "Daddy's golden child, ready to rub his unearned victory in my face."

I roll my eyes. "It isn't me."

He gives me a look. "But you know who it is, don't you?"

"I might," I reply, not giving him a hint of emotion.

"Would you care to disclose it?"

"Disclose what?" a new voice joins us, one that grates on my ears like the wingbeats of a pesky fly.

Hai and I both turn to face Anane.

"What do you want?" I ask at the same time as Hai says, "None of your damn business." Hai tolerates him more than I do, but even he doesn't like to be snuck up on.

Anane crosses his arms. "What? I just asked a question."

"And I'm about to ask you to leave," Hai replies, "and I'm only going to do it nicely once."

Anane rolls his eyes and walks off, flipping Hai the finger on both hands as he does.

Hai mimes slitting his throat.

"You know, maybe I'm still alive because the Charger can't bear to have a child walking around with the title of Agent One," I say, giving Hai a pointed look.

He moves like the wind and has a dagger pointed at my throat, just as I throw up my shielded arm to block it.

The sound of the steel clashing echoes in the Cavern, and I watch as several heads turn our way.

"You take that back," he seethes, his eyes like black fire. "I am not a child; I don't think I ever was. The Charger would be proud to have me as Agent One. I will prove it to you right here and now if I have to."

I grin, even as my arms shake against the force of his own.

Time to ruin his night.

"Silent Night is the new executioner," I tell him.

I watch as the light in his eyes goes out, just for a second, before being replaced by a raging inferno. Still, he lowers his arms and steps away from me, a picture of tranquility on the outside. A total psychopath.

"She will die tonight," he says.

I shake my head. "I can't let you do that."

He looks at me sharply. "Why? Why do you always defend her like you actually care? Why, when you never gave me the time of day?"

I scoff. "As if you ever wanted or needed my limited compassion."

"At least I would've deserved it. She is no one. She is nothing."

I cross my arms. "And yet, the Charger wants her alive."

He clenches his fists and turns away from me, pacing in a small circle as he wars with the demons in his mind. Hai's undying loyalty to our father and his wishes are the only reasons he hasn't ripped Quinn's throat out yet.

Finally, Hai takes a deep breath and turns back to me. "You know he's grooming her to take our place, right?" he says. "It's only a matter of time before he sends her after us, probably once we're too old to fight back properly. We should get her now, when she's young and fragile."

I shake my head. "Not yet, and when the time comes, she will answer to my blade. *I'm* Agent One. I am Father's original prodigy. If anyone has the right to kill her, it's me. You so much as touch her, and I'll tear your fucking heart out."

Even Hai, as well trained as he is, takes a step back from the intensity of my words, but still, he shakes his head in answer.

"I won't deny you your fun, but if you fail, if she kills you like I warned you she will, know that I will laugh upon your grave. The once mighty Kuen, slaughtered by his kid sister who doesn't even know or care who he is."

He turns his back on me then and walks away.

A shudder runs through me, and not for the first time, I wonder which one of us sounds more like our father.

Sephtis

The energy in the room is a living, breathing creature, snaking through the crowds of assassins and climbing up the walls like a shadow of death. I can almost feel the pounding hearts of those standing in the Cavern beneath me, blades ready for the feast to come.

I smile from my perch atop the mezzanine as we all wait for Silent Night's appearance.

Tonight will be the first true test of her skills, the first glimpse of her potential to one day stand at my side, to one day sit in my throne and rule over those beneath her. I have high hopes for her future, but I know the power of patience and planning.

Faith is not enough to keep the world running.

My eyes search the room for my other children, wayward soldiers with feet too small to fill my shoes. Anane is sulking alone in a corner like usual. I find Hai with his knife at someone's throat by the food counter, and then there's Kuen.

My eldest stands stoic as a statue against the far wall, the hilts of two massive longswords sticking up from behind his shoulders. I can't see anything else from my vantage point, but I know he's as well armed as he can be.

Good to know he still has some obedience left in him.

Too bad he's not sharp enough to realize the trick behind my assignment.

I don't need him to keep Silent Night alive, but if he thinks I want him to protect her, he won't try to kill her.

I smile at my cunning just as the Cavern doors open and Silent Night strolls in, dragging her charge behind her with eyes of assassin steel. At least, that's how I imagine it. I'm much too far away to really discern how she feels, but I know I've trained her well. I know her emotions are locked deep within her, if they exist at all.

The energy in the room builds, everyone turning to face her and more trailing in behind, like wolves following the scent of a fresh kill. There is something so fascinating about watching the carnage unfold, seeing how easily people revert back to their ancient, animal nature, knowing that I am the reason their morals have been cast aside in favour of violence and deceit.

It's not easy being the Master Assassin, but the glory is worth the struggle.

Seeing Silent Night now, I know her success will be worth the agony of her retrieval. She will be my best work yet, and when I'm dead and gone, the people of Haven will bow before her or face the consequences of her brilliant wrath.

Kuen

Quinn as the executioner is not at all like what I expected. I tried to picture it earlier, after the Charger told me, but I just couldn't match the face of the girl I'd seen to the cold, emotional mask of the previous man to fill the role. Seeing her now doesn't help.

She saunters into the room like a woman twice her age, dragging a screaming, crying teenage boy behind her like it's nothing, like he is nothing. He squirms and kicks, but her grip doesn't so much as slip. There's an angry, red gash down the boy's face, and the two leave a trail of blood as she continues to the centre of the room, seemingly unaware of the full-grown assassins converging around her.

Quinn is nothing like I remember her.

There is nothing but sadistic satisfaction in her eyes now as she leads that poor boy to his fate, and not for the first time, I wonder what the traitor has actually done.

Is he really a criminal?

Did he truly betray the Guild?

As soon as I start, more questions flood in, questions that I've been subconsciously asking myself for years but never had the courage to answer.

What is the Guild really fighting for?

Will the Charger stop once he destroys the Resistance? Will that really be enough for him?

Why am I here?

What am I doing?

It strikes me then that I don't know the answers, that I don't know if I truly belong here, but I do know that Quinn's current state isn't right. It isn't right to take someone and mould them into whatever you see fit. It isn't right to turn your children into killing machines to fight your enemies and destroy their very soul in the process.

I never knew the difference as a child—I still have trouble now—but Quinn... She had a life, a family, a heart, and now... Now she is indistinguishable from any other Guild Ward. Now she's...a monster.

As I watch her drop the boy to the floor in the middle of the assassin crowd and draw her sword, I finally understand why Trey left, why it was Quinn who changed her so irrevocably. I finally understand why I haven't been able to get her out of my head since I first laid eyes on her seven years ago.

She is a sign, a signal to get out.

Get out while you still can.

Sephtis

The execution is short, but I savour every detail, watch my perfect assassin play her part, revel in the glory as she slaughters those who stand in her way, carving a path back to the doors. I relish the screams of the Guild's latest traitor as he tries and fails to save his life, as his blood spatters on the stained rock of the Cavern floor and his body crumples.

I notice when Kuen walks out of the Cavern without a backward glance, his swords not even drawn, and make a note to visit him when the show is over.

Kuen

My heart is racing in my chest as the Cavern door closes behind me with an echoing thump, like the last page of an ancient, dusty tome. A new chapter of my life is beginning, quite possibly my last, but even as my breaths turn ragged, a strange sense of calm falls over me. For the first time in my life, I feel like I'm doing something right.

I head straight for my room and grab only what I can carry in the pockets of my coats and pants. The red-handled knife Trey gave me for earning the title of Agent One, several cases of ammunition, and the small metal locket with the photo of my mother, something even the Charger doesn't know I have.

I leave the key to my room on the bedpost, not bothering to lock the door, and then I drop into the tunnel beneath my closet. As I shut the trap door behind me, cutting out the last flickers of light, I take a deep breath and let go of everything holding me back.

I am no longer Agent One of the Guild. I am no longer an assassin. And I am no longer the Charger's son.

I close my eyes and picture Quinn again, the hatred in her eyes and the bloodlust in her smile, wishing I could bring her with me, but the Charger would never rest if I stole her from him. I will have to bide my time, come up with a plan, but I will come back for her.

I will come back for you, Quinn. Wait for me. Don't let our father destroy you like he's done the rest of us. And thank you, for waking me up.

The tunnel ahead of me is still pitch black when I open my eyes, but the yawning maw of darkness doesn't deter me. I've walked this path a hundred times, though I will never walk it again.

I take one step then, and another, and disappear into the night.

Sephtis

Kuen's room is empty when I go to see him, his key sitting on his bedpost and the door ajar as if he will return at any moment, but something isn't right. There is a terrible churning in my stomach, a knot starting to form.

He would not walk out of the execution without reason, not when I specifically ordered him to be there. Silent Night didn't need saving in the end—she slaughtered anyone who stood in her way without mercy—but he is not reckless enough to disobey me like that. He must've heard something, seen something even.

I fling open his closet doors, hoping to find clues, but there is nothing within to satisfy the slow panic building in my chest.

Where is my godforsaken son?

If he abandoned his post, I will skin him alive myself, but if someone has done something to him…

My wrath will know no bounds.

I may want him dead, but that is my axe to draw; he is my burden to deal with. My children leave this world when I say so and not a damn second sooner.

I fly out of his room in a flurry of ebony cloak and steel and set about tearing the base apart to find him, while keeping the whole thing under wraps, of course. I can't have people questioning his place as Agent One, or my place as Master Assassin.

I can't have them wondering why I care.

. . .

Three days later, Kuen is still nowhere to be found, and the horrible truth settles in the pit of my stomach, an ugly weight of despair and self-loathing.

He left.

He walked out.

He turned his back on the Guild, and he is never coming back.

It is the only reasonable explanation, though it still makes very little sense. It took me a few days, but I realized that no one could have kidnapped him without a fight, without Kuen leaving a trail of blood or dragging their steaming corpse back to me. I taught him too well to meet his end that way. And even *if* someone had managed to kill him, who would keep quiet about that sort of victory?

No one.

No, my son is not dead. He is not rotting in some Resistance dungeon somewhere. He is gone.

The realization siphons the oxygen out of my lungs. It sends my fist into the wall beside my desk, so hard that my shelf topples over and skulls roll across the carpet at my feet.

He is gone.

My first born. My warrior child. The youngest assassin to ever reach the position of Agent One. Something woke him up; something made him turn his back on me and the Guild and his future. Maybe he was afraid of Silent Night, maybe he sensed his reign would one day come to an end. Maybe I'll never know.

One thing is for certain, though, his departure has left a void in my chest that I will never refill. One more loss to add to my collection. One more colossal disappointment. I punch the wall again, and a tear of pure rage runs down my cheek onto the carpet below.

One day, he will be sorry. He will rue the day he turned his back on me. He will regret not killing Silent Night when he had the chance, because distance will not save his sorry skin.

I will train Silent Night to be three times the assassin he could ever be, to obey me without question, and then I will send her out into the city. I will tell her to hunt her wayward siblings down and bring them back to me for judgment.

I will let them think they have won, and then I will make them eat their poor decisions.

I will destroy them.

I clench my bloody fist, letting the pain distract me from the fury roaring in my veins, and slowly feel my calm, cruel facade return.

Silent Night will be my salvation.

ONE FRAGILE HOPE

Haven City, 08/2111

Blake

The stone wedged in the ground before me is starting to lose its shine after six months exposed to the wind and rain, but the inscription is still as prominent as ever.

Here lies Bast:
A hero, a lover, a brother, and a friend.
Sebastian Xavier Foster
August 2092 - December 2110

The daffodils I picked from my garden to bring here sway in the breeze as I kneel down and lay them up against the face of the stone, slow tears falling silently down my cheeks.

"I wish you were here," I tell him. "I wish you could see what you helped to accomplish. Haven City is…so clean now. The Resistance has returned to living above the surface, the kids are going back to school, and the assassins are almost gone. It's almost unbelievable."

I fiddle with the daffodils, making sure they look their best.

"You did good, Bast. We all did."

As usual, there is no reply, but it feels right to talk to him. I tell myself that as long as I do, he'll never really be gone.

It takes longer than usual to get back to my feet this time, and I can hear both Shirley and Jax scolding me for kneeling in the first place. I run a hand down my swollen belly as I catch my breath.

"Shirley says it won't be long now," I say to the stone. "Our little hellion will be running around the house before we know it."

I try to smile through my tears as I imagine for a brief moment what it would've been like to chase after them with Bast, for the three of us to burst into a fit of giggles when we caught up.

"I was so scared when I first found out, Bast, but Quinn was right. You would've made an amazing father, and I know that wherever you are, you'll always be watching over us."

Another breeze ripples through the cemetery, and I take a deep breath, letting my emotions flow through and then out of me. I miss Bast more than life itself, but I am learning to be okay, to not let his loss cloud the memories, the love and laughter that still radiates throughout me because of him.

Our child will be so loved, and because of Bast, they will grow up in a world free of the Assassin's Guild. They will be safe.

I whisper "I love you" to the stone for the hundredth time, and then I leave the cemetery.

• • •

Jax is finishing up building the baby's crib when I come back from my walk. I never would've been able to fix up the nursery without him and Quinn. They helped patch up the holes in the drywall and paint the walls a cheerful yellow, and we even pulled up the old, stained carpet to reveal beautiful hardwood floors, now partially covered by a rainbow-coloured woven rug, courtesy of Natalie.

The look is finished off with a border of hand-painted stars and clouds, about three feet up the wall. It turns out that Quinn is quite the artist. It's amazing what you can discover about yourself when you're given the free time to try.

"Hey, Blake," Jax greets me when he sees me leaning up against the doorframe. He's kneeling on the floor, fiddling with a crib leg and a screwdriver. "I'm almost done. This last piece is just giving me trouble."

"Take your time," I tell him, coming in to sit down on the rocking chair. "The baby isn't here yet."

"Soon enough," he replies. "You look like a hot air balloon."

I laugh, the action shaking my whole body. "Ow, Jax, you know that hurts." My tone is scolding, but I don't let it reach my eyes.

Still, he winces. "Sorry, I keep forgetting. Man, Bast would've had a really hard time with that."

I manage a smile through the twinge in my heart, and Jax does too. Bast's death impacted us both, but I can't imagine what it would've been like to be the one to pull the trigger. I can still see him opening the door to the control room and bursting into tears at the sight of me. I can still hear his confession, the fear in his voice that I would hate him, but I couldn't.

Bast sacrificed his life to save Jax, and no matter how much it hurt, I understood that because if the roles had been reversed, I would've done the same.

I watch Jax in content silence as he wrestles with the wooden leg and finally gets the crib together.

"There," he says, wiping the sweat off his brow with the back of his hand. "That should do it. The little guy isn't sleeping on the floor on my watch."

"Or little girl," I remind him.

"Or little girl," he echoes. "Did you know in the old days, they used to be able to tell you the gender before birth?"

"I've heard of that, though I'm not sure how they managed it."

He shrugs. "Maybe we'll figure it out again someday."

I smile. "Maybe we will."

Jax brushes his hands together and then gets to his feet. "Could I interest you in some lunch? Quinn tells me I make a mean tomato soup."

I raise an eyebrow. "Oh really? That's not what she told me."

Jax's face falls as he dramatically throws a hand over his heart. "How dare she? After all the hard work I put into it…"

"Hard work my ass," a new voice butts in. "All you do is add water and stir."

I turn around in my chair to find Quinn lounging in the doorway with her arms crossed, a knowing smile on her face.

Jax's face lights up despite her words, and I can't help but smile too at the sight of it. This war tried really hard, but it didn't break us.

"As if you're any better," Jax finally retorts. "If I have to have one more turkey and swiss sandwich, I'm going to lose my mind."

"I'll have you know those sandwiches are gourmet," she replies, "and made with love."

I laugh at that as I get to my feet. "All right, you two, why don't I make us all some lunch, before you start a brawl in my newly finished nursery."

They exchange a quick look, as if weighing their options, and then nod.

I waddle over to the door, Jax falling in step behind me, but halfway there, a flash of pain stabs through my stomach, halting me in my tracks. "Oh God," I gasp. Instinct makes me want to double over, but my bulging stomach stops me from moving far.

Jax and Quinn both rush to support me.

"What happened?" Quinn asks, her eyes wide with trepidation.

"Talk to us," Jax says, his voice serious but gentle.

"I…" Another convulsion wracks through me, cutting off my sentence, and I clench my teeth against the discomfort.

"Blake…"

I take a deep breath once the pain subsides and say, "I think the baby is coming."

Shirley

I'm just about to head out for my lunch break when my phone rings.

"Shirley speaking," I answer. "Who is this?"

"Oh thank God," a familiar voice replies. "It's Quinn. Blake's water just broke, and we don't know what to do. She looks like she's in a lot of pain."

I smile against the phone as I imagine the scene. Blake knows all too well what she's going through, but I doubt Quinn has ever dealt with it before.

"Just take a deep breath," I tell her. "Blake is going to be just fine. She probably has a couple more hours before she goes into active labour. This is only the first stage."

"Active labour? This looks pretty active to me."

I dig my fingers into my forehead. "Okay, never mind that. Is there anyone else with you?"

"Jax is here."

"Good," I reply. "It would probably be best if the two of you brought Blake to the hospital now. Given Blake's history, I don't want to take any chances, but like I said, she has a few more hours at least until the baby comes. Is she able to talk to me?" There's a pause on the line and then Quinn returns. "She's hurting pretty bad right now."

"Okay, well, can you put Ajax on then?"

"What, you don't trust me?"

I roll my eyes. "I'm not dealing with your sarcasm right now, young lady. Give Mr. Forrester the phone, or I just might decide to hang up."

She sighs. "Okay, fine. Jax!"

She yells the last line right in my ear, of course, and I'm holding the phone an inch away from me when Ajax says hello.

"Hello, Mr. Forrester. How are the girls?"

"Quinn's pretty freaked out, but Blake is taking it pretty well. What do you want us to do?"

"I trust you have a wheelchair stowed away somewhere for Blake?"

"Yeah, it's in her downstairs closet."

"And where are you three?"

"Upstairs in the nursery."

"Well then, get her downstairs as carefully as you can, and walk her over to the hospital. Bring the wheelchair with you, but avoid using it unless you have to. It's best for her to walk as long as she can. She's going to be having contractions, but I need one of you to time how long they last and how frequent they are. That'll tell us how close she is. If things start getting worse, call me and I'll meet you halfway."

"Sounds good," he replies. "I'll take care of them."

I smile. "I know you will, and please tell Ms. Ballinger to calm down. She'll only stress Blake out even more."

He laughs. "I'll give it my best shot."

"Then I'll see you soon. Be safe."

"We will."

He hangs up the phone, and I pull a banana out of my lunch bag before setting about getting a room ready for Blake. There are arguably more important tasks on my to-do list, but she has already lost one child on my watch. I won't let it happen again.

Blake

Jax hangs up the phone just as the last of the pain fades. I feel almost fine now, but I know from experience that it won't last. We need to get to the hospital. Now.

"What did she say?" Quinn and I ask him at the same time.

"She's getting everything ready for you and wants us to bring you over."

"Oh thank god," I reply. "Guess none of us are getting lunch."

Jax shrugs. "Lunch is overrated anyway."

"How are we going to get you down the stairs?" Quinn asks, a hint of fear in her eyes.

I scowl. "I can still walk, you know. I'll just need extra support so I don't trip and fall if another contraction comes while we're going down."

She frowns. "What on earth is a contraction?"

I laugh for a second at her naivety, but it's not her fault the Guild taught her about death instead of life.

"A contraction is when your uterus muscles tighten in an effort to push out the baby. Think of it as if it's pulsing but much more violently than, say, a sore muscle throbbing."

She makes a face. "That sounds awful."

"Well, it's certainly not a walk in the park, and it gets worse the longer you're in labour, for obvious reasons."

"Speaking of labour," Jax prompts, "maybe we should get a move on? Quinn is clearly not capable of delivering the baby, and I really don't want to have to learn."

We both scowl at him, but he's right. We're wasting time we don't have.

I take a shuddering breath. "Okay, let's see how far we can get."

They each take an arm, and we walk slowly down the hall to the staircase. Then Jax takes the step below me while Quinn brings up the rear, both ready to catch me if I slip.

I take a couple steps and then pause, trying to control my breathing.

I wish I could see my feet.

It takes us about five minutes to reach the main floor landing, though it feels like ten hours. I stop halfway down for a few minutes as another contraction runs through me. Quinn rubs my lower back while I grip onto the banister like it's a lifeline.

She holds me steady now while Jax grabs the wheelchair.

"You're going to be fine," she tells me. "Jax and I won't let anything happen to you."

I only nod, not trusting my voice. After what happened last time, it's hard to hold onto hope, but I don't want to consider what will happen if this baby doesn't make it. I clench my hands in an effort to stop the tremble starting in my limbs.

"Here we are," Jax says as he returns with the wheelchair. "Do you need anything else before we go?"

I shake my head. "I have all I need here with me already."

The two smile.

"Well, let's do this then, shall we?" he says.

I waddle over to the door just as a wave of nausea washes over me.

"Oh God, on second thought, one of you better grab a bucket."

"On it," Quinn says.

She disappears and then returns a moment later with an empty metal garbage can. "Will this work?"

I shrug. "I hope we don't have to find out, but better safe than sorry."

She nods and sets it in the wheelchair for safekeeping, taking it from Jax so he can come support me.

Jax leads me outside without any further discussion, and Quinn locks the door behind us, tucking the key in her front coat pocket.

I narrow my eyes. "When did I give you that?"

She shrugs. "You didn't."

I shake my head. "I'm in too much pain to argue with you right now, but just know you're going to get an earful for that later."

She grins. "I look forward to it."

I say nothing more and resign myself to the long, painful walk to the hospital, with little to distract me from the thoughts plaguing my mind. I keep thinking about my first child, dead in my arms, about what I did to Deven after, about the look on Jax's face when he told me Bast was gone.

I blink back tears as I try to focus on better memories instead: fighting assassins with Bast and Jax, the look on Bast's face the first time we kissed, shopping with Quinn...

But the memories won't stick and a few tears escape my eyes.

Having a baby is supposed to be one of the most joyous moments of a woman's life, but I can't stop thinking about the horrors I have gone through, all that I have lost.

I can't stop thinking about the fact that if I lose this baby, I will be losing the last piece of Bast that exists in this world.

Shirley

Thirty minutes later, I am pacing the floor of the emergency department, my eyes darting in between the two entrance doors on either side of the waiting area. A small group of patients are watching my progress from their plastic chairs, but I pay them no mind.

Where in God's name are they?

I've had the room ready for ten minutes and have put new gloves on at least half a dozen times, before deciding it wasn't time yet and taking them off. Now I'm wearing a hole in the floor while I give myself whiplash, my mind filling with increasingly more improbable reasons for their tardiness.

What if Blake fell down the stairs?

What if a rogue assassin attacked them?

What if my calculations were wrong and she's out there somewhere giving birth in the street?

I am just about to go out after them when the west doors burst open and the three of them run in. Well, Jax and Quinn do. Blake is very much confined to her chair.

Sweat coats her forehead, and she is clutching an empty garbage bin in her hands, her face half-buried in it. I watch with a grimace as another contraction racks through her and she clenches her teeth in pain.

Jax sees me immediately and wheels her over.

"Where on earth have you been?" I scold him.

He winces. "We came as fast as we could, but we had to take a detour around some debris. Last week's storm must've collapsed this old house. You should've seen it."

I wave a hand. "It doesn't matter. I can take it from here. You two can either head home or wait in here if you'd like, but I must emphasize that the emergency rooms are off limits."

I eye Quinn pointedly as I say it, knowing full well that she's going to either outright ignore me or find a way around my instructions.

As if on cue, her mouth turns up in a frown, and she says, "That's not fair."

"Quinn," Jax tries, but she cuts him off.

"We've been through everything together, and I refuse to let her out of my sight, even for a second."

I raise an eyebrow. "Are you saying you don't trust me, Ms. Ballinger?"

Her eyes widen. "No, that's not it, I just…"

Blake reaches up and grabs her hand. "Quinn, it's okay. I can do it alone; I did before."

"But you shouldn't have to," Quinn replies, tears building up behind her eyes. "You wouldn't be alone if it wasn't for me, and I… I promised him I'd look after you."

A single tear runs down Blake's cheek. "I know," she chokes out. "He knows too. You don't have to keep atoning for your past, Quinn. I forgive you, and I'm not alone. You've been with me every step of the way so far, and I'll know you'll still be there when this is all over. No matter…" She clenches her jaw. "No matter what happens."

Quinn smiles through her tears and gives Blake as much of a hug as Blake can manage. Then she takes a deep breath and says, "We'll be out here if you need us."

Blake smiles too and then turns to me. "I'm ready."

I nod. "All right then, let's deliver you a baby."

Jax hands the wheelchair over to me, and I take Blake back to her room, the weight of my responsibility crushing down on me, though not as heavy as the promise that I would make it right this time.

Blake

As soon as we disappear into the main hospital, my heart starts to race, fearing I'm not ready. I had kept it together with Jax and Quinn because I didn't want them to worry, but with Shirley, I know she'll see right through it anyway. She has a knack for diagnosing problems before you even say anything.

"How are you feeling, Blake?" she asks me then, echoing my thoughts.

"Not the best," I admit. "Pain level is…about a five? And I don't think my blood pressure is too good."

She pats my shoulder. "That's okay. We'll get you sorted out shortly. Just remember to breathe, okay?"

I nod, and the rest of the journey passes in silence as I wade through one contraction after another.

My face is slick with sweat by the time she wheels me into a room, and my jaw is already aching from clenching my teeth. I stretch it open to alleviate some of the pressure, but the stiffness has set in.

A team of nurses bustles in as soon as we enter, and the next ten minutes are a blur. They help me into a nightgown and then onto the bed, whisk the wheelchair away, and set about attaching me to half a dozen machines. All the while, I try to breathe through the pain that is getting stronger and longer by the second.

It's hard to determine whether this is better or worse than the last time, especially since I tried to block the entire memory out after losing her. Still, I can't entirely convince myself that I've gone through this before and that I'm fully capable of succeeding.

Each new contraction feels like a sign of death.

Each minute feels like an eternity.

Each second that passes has me wondering what I'll do if I fail.

<h1 style="text-align:center">Shirley</h1>

In the end, Blake is in labour for ten hours, ten long hours where I swear I don't even look away from her to blink. Each decision and movement is calculated to do what is absolutely best for her and her baby.

We try the pain medication, like before, but she reacts poorly to it once again, so we cut off the supply to that IV and just do our best to make her comfortable. She gets up and walks around the room a few times, as much as she can, and when it comes time to push, she handles it like the seasoned warrior she is. Her eyes betray her fear throughout as she groans and clenches her teeth against the pain, but I can tell from the start that she is stronger than last time, that she's going to make it.

There is nothing worse than trying to deliver a baby when the mother wants to die. There is no determination, no grit or desire to get through the hard parts. We were forced to choose between saving her or the baby the first time because of the circumstances, though I never thought for a second that it was her fault.

This life gives us hardships, gives us tests, and it's up to us to survive them, to learn and grow from them. Losing that child broke Blake's spirit and my heart, that much is true, but the version of us that came back from that dark moment was the version of us that the world needed.

In the end, when I pull the baby into my waiting arms, when I clear their airways and hear their first cries, the struggle is worth it.

Blake

The exhaustion in my limbs is a living thing, unlike anything I've ever experienced before. They say giving birth is easier the second time, but I'm not inclined to believe that, not now. I think, in retrospect, it's best to not lean on anyone's opinions or experiences, because each mother is unique, each story has its own agony and magic.

I lay there breathing slowly in my hospital bed as I wait for Shirley to say something, anything. I don't want to interrupt whatever she's doing, especially if it's important, but the baby's cries aren't enough to convince me they're okay. I need to see them with my own eyes. I need to hold them, no matter what happens.

I almost collapse with relief when Shirley finally walks over, my baby wailing, and clearly alive, in her arms.

"Oh my god," I gasp, tears of joy immediately spilling down my cheeks. "You did it."

Shirley is crying too, her smile trying to surpass the limits of her face. "No, you did it. You fought for your future, and you didn't give up in the face of possible failure. You persevered. I am incredibly proud of you, and I know Bast would be too." She pauses as she walks over to stand beside me. "Now, would you like to hold your daughter?"

My tears fall faster. Bast always said he wanted a girl, if he ever started a family.

I nod, and Shirley passes the baby over, her small form all swaddled in a rainbow-coloured blanket. She feels so small in my arms and yet strong, the heat of her body seeping into my skin, even through the quilted blanket.

She opens her eyes then, golden brown like Bast's, and just stares at me, her cries quieting into a perfect calm. My heart swells.

"Hi," I whisper to her. "Welcome to Haven City, baby girl. You are going to be so loved, my darling. So loved. Your daddy would be besotted with you if he was here, but he's in a better place, waiting for us to meet him when we're ready. He loves you so much."

My tears fall faster then, and I hold her tighter, cradling her against my chest and neck.

The next few years are not going to be easy—life never really is—but I know we will get through it together, that she will be as much my anchor in this world as I will be hers. My little Xavier, ready to conquer the world like her mother or bring sunlight into the darkness like her father.

"My little Xavier," I whisper into her scalp.

My only hope in this world is that I can give her a better life than I ever had, a safer one. It's a fragile hope, in a city still full of uncertainties, but it's an important hope, one I will never give up on as long as I live.

Six Years Later

Xavier's laughter is contagious as she darts between headstones, wanting to be the first to reach our destination. The bouquet of daisies she picked has become rather ragged from her flight, and I smile, glad I brought one of my own.

"Be careful," I chide. "You don't want to twist an ankle."

"I won't," she calls. "Try to keep up."

I shake my head.

So much like her father.

I look up at the clouds, sliding across the skies above like ships on the sea.

You really had to leave me alone with a carbon copy of yourself, didn't you? Is this some kind of payback?

I can imagine his answer, even still after all these years, and that much tells me that I'm in no danger of ever forgetting him completely.

"I win!" Xavier cries out from up ahead.

"Totally unfair," I reply, as I join her a moment later.

She shrugs. "Move it or lose it."

I raise an eyebrow. "And just where did you hear that phrase, little lady?"

She smiles. "Aunty Quinn."

I sigh. "Well, Aunty Quinn and I are going to have to have a talk then, aren't we?"

She says nothing, and together, we look towards the stone. It's a little more weathered now than it was the day

Xavier was born, but his name is still readable, his deeds still remembered.

"Here lies Bast," Xavier recites.

I place an arm around her shoulder and pull her closer to me. "A hero, a lover, a brother, and a friend."

"And a father," Xavier reminds me.

I wipe away a tear that tries to sneak down my face. "And a father," I repeat.

She pulls away from me and kneels down on the grass in front of the headstone, placing her crumpled daisies against the granite. "Happy Father's Day, Daddy. I love you. Mom misses you a lot, but we're okay. Uncle Jax says he's going to teach me baseball, and yesterday, when I beat Aunty Quinn at Go Fish, she swore and threw her cards across the room. I laughed so hard I snorted juice up my nose."

She goes on, telling Bast about her week as I walk over and place my bouquet on top of the headstone and stare out into the city.

She's right; we are okay, and though the pain will never go away, I have learned how to withstand it, to find happiness in the small things, in the here and now with the people I still have. It's been an amazing few years, with many more to come, and though I'm sad he's not here to watch Xavier grow up, I am blessed to have a piece of him here with me, for better or for worse.

I love you, Bast, forever and always.

ONE FIERCE DEVOTION

Haven City, 09/2111

Quinn

The morning sun shines through the sheer curtains around my window as I stare at myself in the mirror, sending a streak of orange across my left cheek. Today is supposed to be a special day—the best day of my life, if you believe the love-struck girls in the romance books Natalie has me reading these days—but there is a weight hanging in my stomach, a feeling of inadequacy.

It is one of those days where I don't feel like I deserve Jax, and though I know deep down it's just my mind being an asshole, I can't seem to shake the feeling.

I've been up since around four in the morning, tossing and turning in the empty sheets. Grandma Marie wouldn't let Jax and I sleep together last night, and quite honestly, it felt like being shot in the foot. It's been months since we've been apart for more than an eight-hour work shift.

Well, after today, you'll never be apart again, I remind myself. *What's one night?*

I sigh.

I can survive one night without sleep no problem, but I can't say the same for my eyes. Blake is going to lose it when she sees me. It's already hard enough to make me presentable with my short hair and pale skin; I didn't need to add dark circles to the list.

My reflection frowns at me as I set about fixing my hair, combing my fingers through it gently to ease out any knots and adjust my bangs. My eyes linger on the space where the blue streak used to be, but the guilt doesn't lance through me anymore. I've made peace with my mother, that much I know for certain.

I wish she could be here to see me today, to see how far I've come, but I know she'll be with me somehow, and that she's never been more proud.

A knock sounds on my door and I flinch out of habit, my hand instinctively reaching for the knife I keep in the drawer of my vanity.

"Are you in there, Quinn? It's just me."

My hand stills as I recognize the voice as Blake. "I'm here," I reply. "Door is unlocked." I listen to the doorknob turn but don't turn around as she walks into the room.

She comes up behind me and gives my shoulders a squeeze. "How are you feeling?"

I meet her eyes in the mirror. "Honestly, I think I might be sick."

She raises an eyebrow. "What are you stressed about now? And if you say you don't deserve Jax one more time, I will give you something worth worrying about."

I wince.

She knows me too well.

"I'm sorry," I reply. "I'm just so full of nerves and the waiting and there's going to be so many people and do we really need a ceremony to know we love each other?"

She gives me a small smile, squeezing my shoulders again. "A wedding isn't for proving you love someone,

Quinn. That's what you did the first year you met. Today is for celebrating that love, for recognizing your perseverance despite the odds and how you chose each other again and again when it would've been easier to walk away. Today is for you, not for anyone else, so don't let anyone steal your moment, okay?"

I take a deep breath and try to relax my stance. "You make it sound so easy."

"Only because you've convinced yourself it's hard. Smile, Quinn. You've got a handsome man waiting for you, and I have a feeling he's not going to take no for an answer."

That finally manages to crack a smile out of me.

Blake smiles back. "There. You can do this, Quinn. After taking down the Assassin's Guild, walking down the aisle should be a mere trifle."

I snort. "It'll be easier than your job this morning, I would imagine. I started on my hair, but I really don't know what I'm doing."

"Don't worry about me; I'll figure it out and we'll have you looking your finest in no time. You just need to sit back and relax."

I roll my shoulders and sit down in the chair Grandma Marie set out for the occasion, trying to slouch a bit. "Where's Natalie?"

Blake reaches around me and grabs a comb from my vanity. "She's just putting the finishing touches on your dress," she replies as she eases the comb through my hair. "She'll be over soon."

I nod and focus on taking slow, deliberate breaths as I watch Blake work.

I'm going to be okay, I tell myself, and I hope that when the time arrives, I can truly believe it.

Jax

I'm pacing the kitchen, probably wearing a line in the tile, when Callum walks in. He glances over at me but says nothing, heading for the coffee maker instead. I continue in silence as the coffee maker goes through its sequence, listening to the whirr of the motor and the slosh of the coffee hitting the mug Callum puts up.

Finally, he slides the mug onto the island and hops up on a stool opposite me. "You want one?" he asks.

I halt in my tracks and lean against the fridge, tapping my fingers against my leg. "I'm good. I, uh, might've had two already."

Callum raises an eyebrow. "How long have you been awake?"

I run a hand through my hair. "I don't know, a few hours? Couldn't sleep."

A hint of a smile crosses his face as he says, "I've never seen you nervous like this."

I scowl. "I'm not nervous."

He shrugs. "Suit yourself."

We exist in relative silence for a few minutes, the only sounds being the sips of his coffee and the faint tapping of my fingers against my arm. My thoughts are a whirlwind in my head, a constant deluge of questions.

Will the ceremony go all right? Will everyone be on time? Is my suit nice enough? Too nice? What if...

What if she doesn't show?

The question is a knife in my gut, and I feel guilty for even thinking of it, but it wouldn't be the first time she's turned away from me. Though she vowed I wouldn't have to wait for her anymore, I know she's still like a scared bird at times. I know she's still afraid it's all a dream and she'll wake up one day back in the Guild, back under Sephtis' thumb, all her struggles and victories having been for nothing.

I know she loves me, but I also know that sometimes love isn't enough.

Callum glances over at me. "Can you sit down or something? You're making me nervous."

I sigh and drift over to the island, taking the second stool and dragging it across the floor to sit across from him instead of beside him. He's become a friend after everything that happened, but sometimes talking to him feels like betrayal, reminds me of the hole where someone else used to sit.

God, if Bast was here right now, he would quite literally slap some sense into me.

A smile tries to form on my lips at the thought, but it's weighed down by the fact that Bast isn't here to share it with me.

Callum gives me a pointed look from across the island that I try to ignore, but his eyes are burning into my forehead, so I take a deep breath and look up. "What?"

"Do you want to talk about it?"

I slouch on my stool. "Not really."

He leans back and crosses his arms. "You know, sometimes you and Quinn are so alike, it's horrifying."

I open my mouth to retort but stop when I realize he's right. I run my hand through my hair again. "It's just… We've come so far, but sometimes I worry it's not far enough, you know? I'm worried I won't do right by her, that I'll be a constant reminder of her past mistakes, or I'll bring up my dead mother in an argument out of spite… What if we can't escape our tragic history? What if we're not meant to be?"

He snorts. "Not meant to be? Jax, after everything the two of you went through together, if it wasn't meant to be, you wouldn't be standing here, stressed about your wedding. If it wasn't meant to be, she would've left you a long time ago, might've maimed or killed you if we're being perfectly honest. If it wasn't meant to be, you wouldn't have bothered to give her a chance. If the two of you aren't meant to be after everything, then there's little hope for the rest of us."

I take a moment to digest his words as my fingers continue their rhythm on the quartz countertop. The rational side of my brain knows he's right, that my anxiety is just grasping at straws and trying to ruin my perfectly good day, but I'm not convinced, not yet.

Callum heaves a sigh and leans back in his seat. "I hate to be the one to say it, but what would Bast say if he was here and you were acting like this?"

My mind conjures up an image of his face, an image I swear sometimes is already fading, and Callum's words finally click. I sigh. "He would tell me I'm being a colossal idiot and that I should stop worrying about it. If Quinnby was going to axe me, she would've done it already."

Callum frowns, but there's a smile behind his eyes. "Are you sure Bast *knew* the meaning of *colossal*?"

I crack a smile then, and the tension falls out of my shoulders as it morphs into a laugh. "He definitely couldn't spell it," I reply when I can breathe again. "God, I miss him so much, man. But you're both right. Everything is going to be fine, and no matter what happens, we'll all be okay."

Callum reaches over the counter and claps me on the shoulder. "That's the spirit. Once Quinn sees you all fancy in your suit, she won't be able to walk away."

I smile. "That's the plan."

"Then let's get started on breakfast and take the day one step at a time. Oh, and I'd probably lay off the coffee if I was you. You'll be sprinting down the aisle at the rate you're going."

I get up to help him with the cooking, and, though it's not Bast at my side, it feels nice to have someone to talk to. Bast wouldn't want me to be alone. He wouldn't want me to push people away simply because they're not him, even if his ego might've suggested otherwise. The man had the biggest heart I know, and even though no one will be able to see him, I know he'll be by my side today.

Quinn

Blake is just finishing up with my makeup when a knock sounds on the door and Natalie's voice calls out, "Knock knock, I've arrived with the masterpiece."

"Come on in," Blake replies as she dusts a brush across my face.

I scrunch up my nose at the unfamiliar sensation. "Are you almost done?"

"Nearly," Blake huffs. "If you would just sit still…"

"Good morning, ladies!" Natalie exclaims as she bursts into the room, her arms full of a big plastic bag that doesn't entirely hide the contents. I see a swath of grey before she shuffles out of sight, likely to lay the dress out on the bed.

"Hey, Natalie," I say, and Blake nods, her eyes narrowed in deep concentration on my face.

Natalie catches my eye in the corner of the mirror, and her face lights up. "Oh my gosh, Quinn, you look amazing!"

I crack a smile. "That's a pretty heavy compliment coming from you."

Blake swats my arm lightly with her free hand. "Keep your mouth closed or your face will be uneven."

Natalie holds a hand over her mouth to stifle her laugh.

Blake continues her job, and Natalie fills the silence with idle chatter until Blake straightens, puts her brushes away, and steps out of the way so I can see myself properly in the mirror.

"Well," she says, coming to stand behind me, "what do you think?"

I study myself in the mirror, the way the makeup heightens my cheekbones and somehow hides the dark spots under my eyes. There's a colour in my cheeks I've never seen before, and yet it looks natural, like that's how it's supposed to be. And my eyes... The mascara on my lashes makes them look bright and more alive than ever.

"Wow, I look..."

"Gorgeous?" Natalie offers.

"Stunning?" Blake adds, giving my shoulders a squeeze.

I look like myself but less tired, less weighed down by the past and the uncertainty of the future. I look... "Free," I breathe.

Natalie and Blake share a smile, and I find myself joining in, the joyful reality of the day finally seeping into me.

"I'm getting *married*," I exclaim, resisting the urge to cover my face with my hands. Blake will kill me if I ruin this makeup.

"Damn right you are," Blake says. "Now, let's get this dress on so we can finish your hair. I cannot wait to see you in it."

"Me neither," Natalie adds. "I hope I did the dress justice."

I turn to her. "It's going to be amazing, Natalie. Better than I imagined."

She beams and runs over to grab the dress, the grey fabric swirling around her as she and Blake help me into it, over my white shift. When they finish zipping me in and smoothing out the wrinkles, I turn to face them and watch as their eyes widen.

"Oh Quinn…" Blake breathes. "Poor Jax won't be able to take his eyes off you."

I smile at her comment, my cheeks heating as I remember the first time she said that to me, before that party in the Den.

"Do you have a full-length mirror in this house?" Natalie asks.

I nod. "In Grandma Marie's room. Why?"

"You have to see yourself." She grabs my arm. "Come on."

Blake follows behind as Natalie all but drags me behind her, the dress fanning out around me as we go. My grandma's bedroom door is open, and we enter the empty space, the mirror leaning against the far wall. Natalie slows and leads me over to it before letting go of my arm. She and Blake watch me as I take in the dress.

If I thought I looked pretty before…

This is nothing like I imagined; it is so much better.

The crimson and grey bodice is in corset style with a heart-shaped neckline, though still modest, and the dark grey skirt flares out, reaching my ankles with its ragged, cut-up ends. I look like a vengeful queen once more, but this time, it feels right.

It's the same dress Blake made me try on all those months ago, when Bast and Jax were on the mission with Trey, after her and I finally made up. Natalie altered it to be longer and more ballgown-like and added a zipper in the back so I could get it on without ruining my makeup.

"Natalie, it's..." I try. I sniff back tears. "God, it's everything."

"Oh, don't cry," Blake starts, her own tears marring her voice. "You're going to make me worse."

I choke on a laugh as I lean my head back and blink my eyes rapidly to dispel the deluge.

"I'm so glad you like it," Natalie says. "It was meant for you."

I nod.

Blake wipes her eyes. "All right, that's enough of that. Let's get you back to your room and do your hair. It's almost time to go."

I take one last look in the mirror before following them out.

Quinn Marie Ballinger, saviour of Haven City, is ready for the rest of her life.

Jax

A breeze threads through the garden, sending the large flowers fluttering like butterflies, though not strong enough to remove their petals. I stand behind the stone wall that cuts the community garden in half, waiting for the ceremony to start, and I can't stop tugging on my tie. For the tenth time in the past seven minutes, I raise up on my tiptoes to peer over the wall at our audience.

Almost a hundred people sit waiting in white plastic chairs arranged in neat rows of ten on either side of a wide walkway covered in rose petals. I wonder if the red carpet beneath her feet will remind Quinn of blood, if she'll wonder like I do how many flowers were sacrificed for their beauty.

I shake my head to dispel the thoughts.

God, what is wrong with me today?

A hand touches my arm. "Hey, are you okay?"

I jump a little at the sudden contact but resist the urge to grab the person and throw them to the ground. Insead, I turn around and find Blake's steady, brown eyes staring into mine. She's wearing a dark red, ruffled dress with shimmery swirls along the skirt. It's simple, and yet pretty.

"Oh, thank god it's you," I say.

She raises an eyebrow. "It's that bad, eh?"

I frown. "What?"

"Jax, you nearly jumped over the wall when I touched you. And I thought Quinn was twitchy today..."

I run a hand through my hair, ruining my earlier attempt to tame it. "Sorry there's just...so many people. I don't know if I can do this."

"Nonsense," she replies. "They're your friends and fellow soldiers—not a single stranger in their midst—and all of them, myself included, are here to celebrate you and Quinn. The two of you are something good that came out of this horrid war. People need to see that happy endings are happening again. You need that happy ending." She pokes a finger into my chest.

I manage a smile. "Yeah, I suppose I do. Callum gave me a pretty good pep talk this morning, but the nerves came back once he left me alone."

Blake squeezes my shoulder and gives me a reassuring smile. "You're going to do great, and just a fair warning, Quinn looks pretty irresistible." She winks at me and then walks off, presumably to take her place in the retinue.

I take a few deep breaths and, for the first time today, try to imagine what Quinn is going to look like. I run through a dozen different dress and outfit options, my brain lingering on a certain red bodysuit more than once, and it helps to keep me calm, though I'm sure none of my guesses are even close.

Then Jenson rounds the corner of the wall, ducking through the arbour. He's wearing a crisp, grey suit, a few shades lighter than mine, and a striped tie.

"Looking good, sir," I tell him.

He shrugs. "I didn't want your future wife to have anything to nag me about."

I smile. "I'm sure she'll find something."

"Probably," he replies, tucking his hands in his pocket. "Well, are you ready then? They've told me it's time."

I brush off my suit and run my hand through my hair one last time. "How do I look?"

"Nervous," he replies, "but it would be wrong if you weren't. It might not feel like it, but you're ready, and I'm certain Quinn will think you've never looked better, regardless."

I let out a breath. "Okay then. Let's do this."

He claps me on the back. "Go make the Resistance proud."

Quinn

My hands tremble slightly as Natalie hands me my bouquet of roses, but for the first time in a while, the colour doesn't make me think of the blood that may or may not always stain my skin. I think of the life ahead of me, the life we all fought so hard to experience. I think of all we lost, but with reverence for once, not despair.

I think of the jokes Bast would make, of the smiles Kuen and Trey would give me, though Kuen wouldn't want me to know he cared. I think of my mother, especially in this garden that I chose because of her. There's tulips galore, lilies and peonies, and flowers she never got the chance to tell me about, but I see her in every petal.

A hand touches mine, and I turn to see my grandma staring up at me, smiling widely from ear to ear. "She's here today, Quinn, and she's never been prouder."

I blink back tears and squeeze her hand. "I know."

Somewhere within the garden, a slow song begins to play, a beautiful harmony of piano and violin. I watch as Blake and Natalie start down the rose petal aisle, and Grandma Marie threads her arm through mine. "Are you ready, dear?"

I nod, not trusting myself to speak.

Then we take our first few steps to the altar, towards Jax and the other half of my heart.

Jax

When I catch my first glimpse of Quinn beside her grandma, walking behind Blake and Natalie, my breath catches in my throat and my heart starts to race.

God, she's stunning, beautiful, more than I could ever imagine or deserve, but somehow, she is mine.

A tear runs down my cheek, and as I wipe it away, I feel Callum's hand dig into my shoulder.

"You're a lucky man," he says.

"Oh, I know," I reply. "Do I ever know…"

I watch her intently as she walks down the aisle with her entourage, until her eyes meet mine and I see the silent promise written there.

You don't have to wait for me anymore.

The tears fall faster, and when Grandma Marie passes her hand into mine, and Blake and Natalie take their places at her side, I see she's crying too.

"You're beautiful," I breathe.

She smiles. "I could say the same about you."

I squeeze her hands in mine, and she matches my intensity. We stare into each other's eyes as the music fades and Jenson begins to recite the ceremonial words.

Quinn

My heart feels like it's going to burst out of my chest as I stand hand in hand with Jax and listen to Jenson recite some ceremonial jargon. It takes a great amount of effort to keep myself from rushing through the words when Jenson finally turns to me.

"I, Quinn, take you, Jax, to be my husband, to have and to hold, from this day forward, to fight for us no matter what obstacles stand in our way, to love and cherish forever."

I don't take my eyes off Jax as Jenson says, "Ajax Forrester, do you take Quinn to be your wife, till death do you part?"

"I take her as my wife until our souls are particles in the dust of time," Jax replies.

Fresh tears run down my face, and I catch a glimpse of Jenson's smile in the corner of my eye.

"Then I pronounce you husband and wife," he says. "You may kiss the bride."

I can hear the crowd cheering in the background, but all I can feel is Jax as he lifts me into his arms and our lips meet. We kiss like we've never seen each other before, like we've just reunited after nearly losing each other forever, like we have all the time in the world, and I suppose we do.

ONE FADING MEMORY

Haven City, 05/2129

Quinn

I'm peeling potatoes in the kitchen for dinner when I hear the front door slam shut.

"Mooom, I'm hooooome," Molly's voice calls out, and I smile.

"Don't leave your shoes in the walkway," I remind her. "Your dad used some choice words last night when he tripped over them."

"Got it," she replies.

A few minutes later, she walks into the kitchen and hoists herself up onto the island stool. "What's for dinner?"

I gesture to the cutting board. "Potatoes."

She frowns. "Is that all?"

I shrug. "Is that not enough?"

She raises a black eyebrow. "Well, if that's all we're having, you're going to need a lot more potatoes. Jean eats a lot."

I laugh at that. "He's a lot like your uncle that way, always thinks better with a face full of food."

Molly's returning smile is wistful. "I wish I could've met him."

"Me too, kiddo," I reply, turning back to my potatoes. "And I was joking—we're having chicken and peas too, if I don't screw it up."

Jax usually cooks dinner, due to my absence of decent cooking skills, but I'm in between assignments and have the week off, so I am trying to surprise him.

"You'll do fine," Molly assures me.

"Hmmm," I say, pulling more potatoes out of their bag. "Where is your brother anyway? He better not have been held back at school."

"He's fine," she replies. "He went to play with Samuel at Aunt Natalie's."

"I suppose that's acceptable."

The two formed a tight bond over the years, being the only boys in the family aside from Jax and Callum. Sam is Natalie and Cal's youngest at ten years old, and she joked during our shared pregnancy that at least the two would be buddies.

Jax and I were the last of our group to have kids, so we had worried our child would be left out at first. Of course, we soon found out I was having twins, but it didn't matter. Molly, Jean, and Sam get along quite well, and when Molly grows tired of the boys' shenanigans, she can always hang out with Gwen—Natalie's youngest daughter—instead.

"You didn't want to go with him?" I ask Molly as I dice the last of the potatoes.

"They were talking about building their robot car, and besides, I have homework."

"Oh? What kind of homework?"

"Well... We, uh... We started learning about the Guild War today."

I drop my knife at her words, and it clatters into the sink. I don't know why it shocked me so much; I knew this time would come, and I'd already discussed my past with her cousins three times over, but somehow... Somehow, I thought I could keep it from her and Jean forever.

"Mom, are you okay?" Molly asks me.

There's concern in her voice, and I take a deep breath.

Get it together, Quinn, I tell myself. *You survived a war and a life as an assassin. Surely you can survive telling your daughter about it.*

"Yeah, I'll be okay," I reply. "Just give me a minute."

I grab a pot out of the drawer at my feet and fill it halfway with water. Then I pick the knife up out of the sink and use it to scrape the potatoes into the pot. I set the pot on the counter and then turn to face Molly.

I brace myself against the island as I say, "What do you want to know?"

"Only what you want to talk about," she replies. "I know you and Dad were in the thick of it from what you've talked about, but today... My teacher said a woman named Quinn Ballinger is to thank for the peace we have now. Is that... Are you that Quinn?" There is both excitement and trepidation in her voice, and I'm not sure which makes me more anxious.

I sigh. "Firstly, I didn't win that war on my own, if that's what your teacher was implying. I could not have done it without your father, without Aunt Natalie and Blake, and certainly not without Uncle Callum and Bast.

Secondly, there was a long time where I didn't want to save Haven at all."

Molly frowns. "Why not?"

"I was a bit misguided and, well, on the wrong side at first." I take another deep breath and roll up my sleeves. "You remember what I told you about these tattoos?" I ask her, running my fingers over the ink.

There's been many times over the past decade where I've considered getting rid of them, but I can never bring myself to do it.

Molly nods. "All the names of the people you want to remember?"

I force a smile at her words. She was only five when she first asked about them, and while she wasn't ready for the whole story then, I couldn't let myself lie about it.

"Yes," I reply. "I never told you why I want to remember them, did I?"

She shakes her head.

I walk around the island and take the chair next to her, and she half turns in her seat to face me. "This story isn't a happy one, love," I tell her, "but it's true. I grew up in the Assassin's Guild after my mother was murdered by the Master Assassin. I became an assassin myself, and these…" I touch my tattoos again. "These are the names of all the people I killed, starting from when I was just your age. I kept every single one because despite my upbringing, despite the way the assassin ideals were tortured into me, there was always a part of me that knew what I was doing was wrong, and I didn't want to forget myself."

For a minute, Molly says nothing, just stares at my ink like she's never seen it before. I brace myself for the rejection, for the fear, but I flinch when Molly takes my hand in hers and squeezes it instead. "It's okay, Mom," she tells me. "It must have been hard."

I let out a breath and try to relax as my brain hyper-fixates on the feeling of her hand in mine. Only my daughter would be brave enough to hold my hand after being told I was a killer. "The hard part was that, a lot of the time, it was extremely easy. Deaths blur together. Killing becomes second nature. The blood on your hands is washed or worn away. For a long time, I was lost. For a long time, I was able to convince myself I enjoyed what I did."

She looks up at me. "What changed?"

"I was originally told that the Resistance was responsible for my mother's death, but when I found out the truth, I switched sides. I became eager to enact my vengeance, to kill the Master Assassin and take the Guild for myself, but then I met your father." I manage a smile. "He challenged me, all my beliefs and my trust issues and even my ambitions. He challenged me to become a better person and slowly, I did. I realized that what I truly wanted was my freedom, and I turned into the woman that saved Haven City."

I squeeze Molly's hand back and then she lets go. "It's a long story, isn't it?" she asks me.

I nod. "It's a story that almost ended horribly more times than I can count. The road to salvation wasn't easy, and I did some truly horrific things, but I try to believe that in the end, I was on the good side."

She smiles at me. "Of course you were on the good side. My teacher called you a hero."

"Then she's a very kind woman," I reply, "but I want you to remember, Molly, that heroes have darkness inside them too, just like any person. It's just about what they do with it. In the end, I fought darkness with darkness and won. Sometimes, I wonder if I could've won with just the light. We'll never truly know, but I try to be better every day."

"I believe in you," Molly says. "I'm not scared, if you're worried about that."

"That's good," I reply. "I was worried a bit, but I think when I first brought you and your brother into the world that I was more worried about rubbing off on you, that my past would come back to haunt us all." I reach out and run a hand down her long, dark hair. "I'm more than relieved to see that my fears were all for naught. You two make me so proud every day."

She beams and leans forward for a hug.

I wrap my arms tight around her. I still haven't broken the habit of hugging people like it's the last thing I'll do or the last time I'll see them. Out of all my lingering quirks, I don't think this one is so bad.

When Molly pulls away, I grab her shoulders gently and say, "I want you to know, though, that even if you stray from the good path, I will still be here for you, no matter what. There is nothing you can do that will make me love you less. I might get angry, I might be disappointed, but I will never give up on you. So don't you ever think that you're alone. Okay?"

"Okay," she says.

"I can tell you more later," I tell her, "but right now, I think I need to finish dinner. Your dad will be home soon and if I don't have the chicken in the oven, he'll be tempted to take over."

"Can I ask him about it too?" she asks, her eyes trailing after me as I get up from my stool and walk back over to the sink.

"Of course you can, honey," I reply. "Just be gentle and maybe avoid asking about Uncle Bast for now, okay? Your dad didn't have as hard a time as I did, but his wounds still run deep. War affects everyone; some people just happen to have more noticeable scars." I tap my metal leg for emphasis.

She nods, and the next fifteen minutes pass in comfortable silence as I peel and slice carrots and then start on the chicken. Molly grabs a notebook and pencil from her backpack and starts scribbling furiously, presumably noting down what I said for her homework. The scratch of her pencil is soothing.

Eventually, she sets the pencil down and says, "You know, Mom, you should write a book."

I frown. "What about?"

"Your story, duh."

"Oh, well, I don't know, honey… It's pretty complicated, and I don't think anyone would want to read it. I don't think I'd want them to either."

"But my teacher says history is important. We lost so much during the Guild Wars. It would be cool to have a book about it written by our hero."

I smile at that. "I'm not a very good writer."

"You could learn! I can help you, if you want."

"I'll think about it, okay?" I say, trying to placate her.

She sighs. "When grown-ups say 'I'll think about it,' they really mean 'no.'"

I snort. "That is so not true."

"Whatever you want to believe, grown-up," she replies with a shrug.

I shake my head and continue with dinner as she does her homework in the background.

When did she become such an inquisitive young lady?

Watching her and Jean grow up has been fascinating to me, even after watching their cousins before them, because all their milestones were so foreign. I never had my first day of school, never had ribbons for good marks, never celebrated my tenth birthday.

The first birthday I celebrated after my mom's death was my twentieth, after grandma Marie told me I was born October 23, 2091. Even knowing my birthday after so many years in the dark felt like an accomplishment. Now, my children get to live the life I never had. They don't have to live in fear of being attacked in their sleep. They don't have to focus on surviving day in and day out. They don't need to work on their physical fitness like their lives depend on it.

And when I think about that, despite my lingering trauma, I know I've won. Despite the nightmares that still rage and the way I jump when someone accidentally startles me, I know it's all worth it. Sephtis may have left marks on me that will never truly fade, but he will never touch my children, and for that, I am grateful.

• • •

That night, I'm sitting at the desk in my library on the third floor, brushing aside the piles of canvas rolls and paint pots as I crack open a notebook I stole from Molly's room. I clench the pencil in my hand as I stare at the blank page.

Molly's words have been digging into me ever since our conversation.

History is important.

I kept my tattoos so that I wouldn't forget the people I killed, the lives I ended, but I never thought about how I was supposed to remember my story, how I was supposed to pass on my knowledge so future generations wouldn't make the same mistakes.

I understand now why people used to write books — to make a mark on the world in an otherwise boring life, to entertain people and help them escape from their woes, but most importantly, they did it to pass on their knowledge so future generations wouldn't make the same mistakes. People don't live forever, but words can, ideas can.

There will come a day when no one remembers me or my story, but they'll be able to read about it.

I take a deep breath and pen the first words across the page, feeling a weight lift from my shoulders as I start to empty my brain of the baggage I've been carrying for far too long. I start at the beginning, the only beginning that truly matters anyway.

The stupidity of humanity never ceases to amaze me. They all must have a death wish. Well, I'll consider myself a genie, but they'll have to get in line…

AUTHOR'S NOTE

Thank you so much for reading!

If you liked *Assassins Below*, it would mean the world to me if you could leave a review on Goodreads and/or your chosen vendor. Reviews feed authors and I can't wait to hear your thoughts. Even a rating by itself or a single sentence can help boost rankings.

If you are interested in more content from yours truly, please subscribe to my newsletter. I send monthly updates on writing, releases, and more, as well as newsletter exclusive giveaways and bonus content. You can sign up on my website which I have left below. I can't wait to share more with you!

www.emmacouetteauthor.com

ACKNOWLEDGEMENTS

I'm going to try to keep this one short, as befitting a book of this size. In truth, I'm thankful again to everyone who touched the Guild Trilogy because *Assassins Below* wouldn't exist at all without the success of its predecessors.

I want to thank my boyfriend Allan for his unwavering support of my author career, my critique partner Ashley for her enthusiasm and advice for these stories, my editor Nicki for diving into this world yet again, and my cover designer Miblart for the stunning job on another cover.

Thank you as well to the wonderful members of my cover reveal team–Alina, Stephanie, Sandy, and Robin–for spreading the word about this book and building excitement.

I also want to give a shoutout to Hannah Richards and Pagan Malcom for their Booked program, and

Kathyrn Marie of Sapphire Ink Press for organizing another amazing book tour.

Last, but never least, I need to thank my readers. Thank you for embracing this story, this world, and these characters. Thank you for giving a young assassin a chance and following along on her journey to the end and beyond. I hope these extra stories brought you some closure, like they did for me, and if you ever have questions about how our friends are doing now, send them my way.

ALSO BY EMMA K. C. COUETTE

ABOUT THE AUTHOR

Emma Couette **is** a Canadian wordsmith whose second passion is wood working. She has written a few award-winning short stories and dabbles in poetry when the inspiration strikes her. Her dreams include travelling the world, being a mom, and owning a small library. *Assassins Below* is her first short story collection, a companion to the Guild Trilogy.

Website: www.emmacouetteauthor.com
Instagram: emmacouetteauthor
Facebook: emmacouette.10
Tiktok: emmacouetteauthor
Twitter: ecouetteauthor